The Hero of Houston

Connor Kerns

Published by Connor Kerns, 2024.

This is a work of fiction. Similarities to real people, places, or events are entirely coincidental.

THE HERO OF HOUSTON

First edition. March 8, 2024.

Copyright © 2024 Connor Kerns.

ISBN: 979-8224581399

Written by Connor Kerns.

Chapter 1: Time for a Reckoning

The sun burns hydrogen, but it doesn't explode. On earth, the unexploded hydrogen bombs lurking in the dark are more powerful than the bomb dropped on Hiroshima, which devastated 47 square miles and killed hundreds of thousands of people and millions of living creatures. But think of Houston's hydrogen tanks, sticking up in plain sight: now, if those tanks exploded—!

Pat Steadson junked the 'hydrogen' message. He was pissed—either it had been cleverly camouflaged among all the kudos, or he had been distracted by the afterglow of the afternoon. Or he'd automatically opened the next message while he was waiting and waiting for the damn phone call...

Yep, the day's sweet excitement sure was turning to sweaty vexation. Going from high to low, bang. Dang. Goddamn. And somewhere down the road, a loud machine was pounding-banging away, for who knows what reason.

He *Don't-Disturbed All* except 'Family'. And looked through the car window at Houston's hazy blue sky, streaked with a single white vapor trail. And, the banging got louder. Still, God and the heavens were up there. Regardless of the plastic smart squirming in his moist, squeezing hand. He told his hand to relax. He nodded—he could be patient, he could deal with vexation.

Yep, even though everything was getting moist, including his pits. Somehow the Gulf humidity had penetrated the extra-thick glass and was busy defeating the A/C. A sun sliver pierced his eye, reflected off the side mirror. Like someone was screwing with him down here, picking the cherry off his triumph. He snapped on his sunglasses and wiped his hand on the seat. The unseen machine stopped banging, and he breathed a sigh out.

Through the privacy screen, Tuck's mouth was moving. The new driver's head bobbed up and then settled again—jabbed by one of

Tuck's snarky comments? Possibly. Two men killing time in the turnout while their big boss in the back seat was waiting for a personal phone call that was five minutes late. Clearing the way for a few empty minutes...couldn't Pat consider it a gift?

He looked around. Above the top of the sunglasses frame he could see the vent air teasing his thick bangs. Clumps rose, fell, and rose higher, mounding into the fin shape that made him look foolish during the first gubernatorial election. Immediately, the fateful GIF throbbed in his memory, and he dismissed that by repeating to himself three or four times, 'Nobody's fool.' Goddamn negativity.

Leo's call was now seven minutes late. Despite the cold air and soothing mantra Pat's face felt hot. Dread replacing vex? No, he wouldn't let it be dread, no. Squeezing his muscles, a familiar anger swaggered out, his body snapped backward and he pressed down his hair with one hand and, at the same time, tightened his grip on the smart with the other hand and pumped it in the air while the screen flashed the time—eight minutes late. The plastic notches pinched his fingers but the darn thing still inched upward no matter how tightly he gripped it—like it had a life of its own.

'Call!' He almost said it out loud. The word repeated in his head and offered no relief and he worried the thing could explode under the crushing pressure of his fingers, so he lowered his beating arm and tossed the smart down on the seat. He gasped a little, grateful no one could see him in such a state. Like an old enemy, internal pressure crept up as seconds passed, swelling and pushing, the seconds straining one by one until a wild string of words spewed out of his mouth and ended with, "Shit-Goddamn!"

Shit. Hadn't sworn out loud since he'd made the vow at Marta's funeral. Silent swearing was okay, but out loud, even in a soundproofed car....'Marta,' he thought, 'Losing control.' Involuntarily, he leaned and looked forward, even though he knew driver and lieutenant couldn't hear through the one-way glass; he also knew the dark side windows kept anyone outside the car from seeing him clearly. He checked anyway, scanning in a wide arc to make sure no one was near the car. He liked to be sure of things; he kept his eyes open; he'd been in plenty of scraps. His face and hands felt swollen and uncomfortable, even though the climate display read 71 degrees. A strangled, frustrated sound erupted in his throat. Instead of allowing any more profanity out, he repeated, "Nobody's fool" aloud several times. The seconds dripped by so slowly.

At this point, one part of his brain started making excuses for his feelings: this wasn't dread or anger but excitement left over from the day; of course he was fired up for doing big things and that was good and he didn't need anybody's help; plus, God wouldn't mind one small 'shit' from a guy who was ready to charge up the world, no, Sir, and he wasn't dreading talking to Leo, he was optimistic. Yep, today was very big, even if he was just parked on the side of a side road waiting for his smart to ring. Putting his name in the hat spontaneously, without warning anyone about it, had been so darn satisfying! Yes, Sir. So unlike the way the newbie sycophants would do it! He looked away from the younger men in the front and scanned out the rear window, feeling a smile tighten his cheeks—'Enjoy each part of it.' Nothing to be seen out the back but a fence and brown land sloping down to a brown line which, somewhere beyond, marked the Atlantic Ocean. The landscape blurred as his focus drew inward so he could re-live the thrilling sequence after the speech...

...claps, hoots, piercing whistles. Grating Question from the East-Coaster: "What about the health effects, Governor?" 'Ozone,' his brain replayed—he wished he understood chemistry better—but keep it simple—Answer: "You've got to pay to play." "But the climate disaster—" Cut that off quick: "The sky wasn't falling yesterday. It's not falling today." New Guy, leading question, nice work by Props: "Policy-wise, wasn't President Scott your hero?" "One of them, yes. And Immortal Morrill. And, our First Lady of Texas Mizz Ima Hogg—"

not too condescending of a 'That's-for-the-ladies' wink. New Guy loses bonus points for awkward, obvious, rushed follow-up: "Would you consider running for President?" Oh well, awkward or not, it's the opportunity: "If America needs a man like me, darn right I would." Applause washes away the awkwardness, more applause, violent pounding-stomping-whistling-cheering! And then all the kudos…!

But the other part of his brain called 'bullshit'. He sensed the smile on his lips shrinking away. Okay, he could be elated that the news would spread like the wildfires all over the west. But should he be so optimistic he could break out of the Party cage? The suspense of not knowing, not having enough influence. Here he was, trapped between the July heat and the fake cold air from the car with the darn smart next to his bucking leg, fretting like a nervous kid. He was fretting! He was scared!

He stopped his leg's jiggling. The other part of his brain piped up again. 'Don't be negative. The speech! The spontaneous words…' But it wasn't spontaneous, was it. Nothing was. Everything had been planned out and then didn't work the way he wanted it to. 'Bastards everywhere, inside and outside, ready to strike. Marta…' Oh how he wished Marta—

The lieutenant's head turned slightly, tongue flicked: a snake in a suit with gossip for lips. The driver's head jerked and nodded. Probably antsy to get on to the hotel. The schedule, we're behind schedule! No doubt the Party wanted to book conferences and strategy meet ups and donation signings and trumpet the significance of his birthdate on New Year's Eve, and throw parties and…all that darn hoo-ness. No doubt they couldn't abide his delay arriving at the hotel. No. 'People can wait, they can live with do-not-disturb for thirty minutes!' The big silver car—S.U.V., really, though he always thought of it as a car—stayed put, under his orders. Yep.

Outside, the haze was thickening, like the blue afternoon had blown up and gone somewhere else. He flicked the A/C louvres so the air hit his face. Then he combed his hair with his fingers, combed again, again...the motion was soothing, and it calmed down the thick hair. Why did he let stuff turn him into a furnace? He sat back. Music must've come on inside his head because he was tapping the smart in rhythm; good beat; old song from high school; steady. He wanted to give all his attention to Leo instead of to the two pawns inside the car and the twenty-nine million people of Texas outside it. Anxious chaotic humanity, clogging up the state. Clogging up his mind.

Don't let them. Yep, this was his time spreading out right now, this was family, this mattered. Yes, Sir. This was his granddaughter, darn it anyway, bullied! He punched repeatedly just above his knee. Jesse had fought the new school every step of the way; what if Leo was late calling because Jesse had taken her back to T.E.P.? Contingency: what would he do? Darn, he was too riled to analyze—never mind, he'd shoot from the hip, he'd know what to say...but!...but Jesse better not defy him.

That triggered a puff of frustration, eyes squinting, hand flicking. He saw the lieutenant's head turn again, a flashy fat new smart going up to his ear. Pat grinned—someone's calling him about the schedule, right now! Amused, he sat back and let his arms widen; the wet clinging to his pits was drying up. 'Nobody's fool.' The mantra finally sank in, and he relaxed deep into the cool leather.

The seat smelled earthy-good and took him back to tightening the strap on Rex. Other high plains smells followed—sweat, grass, pine, creek bed flint. More sensations mixed in—snow scattering, creek bubbling, horse grunting on jumps, hawk keering. How long since he took a ride? He thought back—before the first campaign, even before the trouble dragged him back to Jasper—six years, he shouldn't have sold the old house, he knew he'd get stuck in Austin, and once Marta was gone Laird would always make an excuse to skip a family trip—

A knocking on the privacy window jolted him. The lieutenant was waving and signaling 'high priority' just as the smart vibrated and Jesse's number flashed and Leo's face smiled up at him from the screen. Pat's body revved to life like an engine. He buttoned the car speaker, "I'm taking this call," and buttoned off before the lieutenant's voice could do more than make a guttural, "Nuh—"

Pat's heart thumped as he tucked the plastic next to his ear, and, pumping all the warmth he could into his voice, he smiled and said, "Hiya, T., how was school?"

Leo's piping voice replied, "Okay I guess Grans."

"Oh-kay?" He teased a little, "Just oh-kay? Okay how?"

"It was okay...okay." His granddaughter's voice sank a bit, not defeated but not enthusiastic, either. He nodded to himself—fourth grade, awkward, pecking order, the year he'd had to muscle his way up; but little girls...he wasn't sure about the range of conflicts they suffered. Marta hadn't ever talked about her girlhood. Bullying boys you could beat up; but this bullying girls thing...out of his territory. The school counselors had said it was 'normal' for girls to play mind games. 'Normal—what did that mean, Marta?' He saw his wife's face, saw her lips forming the word, 'Patricius', but her ghost gave no answer to his question. He was on this campaign trail alone. What he *did* know was that darling wispy Leo, with her gentle face and small hands, wasn't going to have to punch her way to the top.

"Did you make any new friends?" he asked, a little teasingly.

"Grans I don't know anyone at that school."

Blunt, truthful—as always. Lord he loved this kid. "I know Pretty Miss, but maybe there were some girls you thought were nice?"

"We didn't play outside they said it was too smoky." She sniffled.

"You crying?"

"Not crying. My nose is running."

"Must be allergies." He'd have to make sure she saw an allergy doctor. Who *wasn't* allergic to smoke, though, for God's sake?

"I guess," was all her answer.

He wasn't sure what to say next—that sandpaper-like chafing in his brain when a child didn't know how to respond to an adult discussion. Marta would say, 'Try talking her language.' But they had raised boys, not girls. He suffered from a...paucity—where did that word come from? Marta, the eternal schoolteacher: 'Patricius, you got...paucity when it comes to children.' Yep, lacked the lingo—there was another word Marta used but he couldn't remember—anyway, lingo was good enough, he didn't know Leo's lingo, that was the long and short of it.

"What else happened today?" he managed, aware of the gap in their talk. "You have piano today?"

"Yes."

"What're you playing?"

"Beethoven."

"Wow, what did you say, Button? Darn, I can't believe your fingers can play all those big notes." He laughed. "I can't wait to hear it. Beethoven now, you're getting awfully advanced. What's-what're you playing, what's it called?"

"Sonata...." Her voice dipped and he strained to hear.

"T., speak into the receiver, I can't hear you, okay?"

"I said math. The teacher made me stay late." Now she sounded low.

He tried to lift her up, elongating the words gently: "She did? And why is that now?"

"He."

"Oh, sorry, I thought your new teacher was a woman."

Something inaudible. Noisy breath out. Then, "Will you light the rest of my sparklers with me?"

"Course I will, I'll come over this weekend, okay, we'll do it!"

"Okay. I want to—"

The rear passenger door popped opened—Pat realized Tuck had opened it—the whiny voice overwhelmed his granddaughter's: "Guv, we got a bomb threat in the Petro Patch!"

His lieutenant's scowling face was poking inside his private world, polluting it with hot air and bad breath and bad news. Mute. "I'm on a call, get out." Tuck's tongue flicked in and out and then the man pulled back but didn't shut the door. Pat slid across the seat, opened the other door and strode away from the parked vehicle—unmute—"Sorry Pretty Miss." He was approaching a fence at the side of the road. "Grans got interrupted." Bomb threat, right, tell me another screwy one, Tuck. "What kind of math problem?" There was a pause. "T., you still there?"

"I want to go back to my old school, Grans," the voice said, small and very low.

"Oh, Leo, I know this is hard. I know that, but you're getting to be a big girl and it was just the first day. You'll be behind on some things but forwarder on others. Schools aren't the same. Things get easier after you get to know the lie of the land. Tomorrow will be better, and the next day better after that."

"Na-Na would let me go back."

He felt a stab in the chest: Marta's sweetness, the wretched melting of it away, the bitter little girl who sounded like Marta while invoking her. Okay, yes, maybe Marta would have argued for it. "T., I wish Na-Na was here so we could ask her, but she isn't, you know. You have to be a brave girl, okay?"

There was a pause, some muffled sounds.

Then, Leo's voice came back with a sense of finality, "Mom wants to talk to you."

"I love you, you're gonna make it through this just fine, okay?"

An indistinct sound was heard, then Jesse's breath preceded her voice. "Hi."

"Hello, Jesse. Was it rough?"

"I believe so." He could hear his daughter-in-law's flat resistance to the change. He sensed she stood poised to mete out another round of punishment for forcing the move; not unlike Party members who sought to appease instead of digging in and fighting and blaming you for all the unpleasantness it involved. Some people just couldn't come at you straight; they couldn't see that it's always about the means. Leo shot straight, Marta too. But Jesse...she was veiled or came sideways. He couldn't lecture her about justifications, however.

He waited but she wasn't saying more, so he pitched, "It was her first day, Jess, it'll get better."

"I presume you heard her."

"What do you mean?"

"I mean she wants to go back to Episco."

"Not after one day," he said firmly.

"That's what she says she wants."

"Now, Jesse, we had this fight already." He tried to conciliate, using the tactic of seeming to beg forgiveness: "This is the best thing for Leo and if it's not, I'll take the blame, but we're not going to know in one day. Correct? It's one day. Episco is not a good place after what happened to her." He repeated his mandate: "I will not have my granddaughter bullied."

"I didn't know you knew so much about kid bullying, Mr. Steadson." This irked him. Jesse wasn't the smartest woman or the prettiest; tall, almost regal, certainly; but why his son had married her was baffling to him. Marta was beautiful, why wouldn't he find a beautiful woman, a real partner—smarter than him, even. But his son deliberately married a...not a stupid woman but a limited one...not clever but sly. Jesse seemed to harbor a mean desert scavenger inside her stately body—sniffing around for bones to suck on.

"Me?" he challenged, a tactic he liked to use to get people to back off.

"Bullying has increased in the last two years, you know."

He could hear she was holding fast; he tried humor, "Now, now, I'm the Governor of Texas, did you miss my first term? You think our Party would have invested in me if I couldn't hold my own?"

"Kid bullying." Humor was often tough with Jesse—she usually went literal. "I said I didn't know *you* knew so much about kid bullying." Not backing off, he heard it in her voice, creating a strange pang in his guts; it hurt, and it wasn't just the attack on him, the bullet *'you'* striking him low down. There was something else, a secret she'd dug up: yes, he sensed other trouble.

He upped the warning by asking softly, "What point are you making, Jess? Go on, spell it out."

However, judging from the muffled sounds, his daughter-in-law was talking to Leo, something about opening the door.

"Sorry," she said a moment later.

"Is Laird back?" he asked.

"Just now."

"Put him on."

"I'll tell him to call you, Mr. Steadson," Jesse had turned up the southern sweetness in her voice, "We're all at sevens at the moment."

"Jesse, please, do what I asked." He saw Tuck's interfering hand in his peripheral vision—Mr. Self-Importance was interrupting him, maneuvering between him and the fence, between him and his personal life, waving, face frantic. "Hold on!" Mute.—"Tuck, this is a private call."

"But it's an emergency—!"

"*This* is an emergency!" he shouted so loudly his ears rang. "*This* is a family emergency, okay!?" Quieter: "Now let me handle it in private." Tuck's tongue worked again and his jaw did a silent grind, and he threw up his hands and said something about hell to pay and stalked back toward the car.

Pat held up the smart and tapped 'unmute'. "Jesse?"

"Howdy, Dad. Boy, you can cause trouble, can't you." Laird's voice was broad and warm, the perfect sales instrument.

"Hi-do, Laird. Is Leo really in bad shape?"

"She'll get over it, you know, she's young."

The familiar cavalier response; Pat dismissed his son's optimism. "Now, Laird. Listen to me. Don't let Jesse send her back to that other school."

"Nothing to worry about."

"Laird, don't say that." He softened his tone. "I mean Jesse always gets what she wants out of you. Correct? Why shouldn't I worry?"

"Everything's fine, Dad, it's just a school. One school's good as the other."

"No they aren't and you know it."

"I mean Episco is no better than this one, Fuss, Fess, whatever it's called."

"F.A.S." Pat shook his head, visualizing his son's easy shrug, the one that Marta always warned about: 'Don't let that boy bamboozle you.' "F.A.S. is better no question, Laird. Facts are facts and that's that."

"Well good."

Pat hated that mindless expression. But he asked lightly, "Anyway, how's P.J.?"

"How should I know, I just walked in."

"Where were you?"

"Some kale city in Oregon. I do not know why people get so excited about trash."

"Business is good, though?"

"Not bad, considering."

"You saw my speech?" Pat was aching to know what Laird had thought. Hah—always wanting his oldest son's approval; he suspected Laird knew that and gave it reflexively.

"No, I can't watch on the plane, I fall asleep. I'll catch it later, can't wait. Hey, Jesse's after me about something. I better—whoa, there, partner!" P.J.'s rambunctious happy giggles could be heard in the background.

Pat smiled through disappointment and said, "Okay, well, you better wrassle that steer, and give him a kiss from me. Keep Leotie—" The machine banging resumed, louder than ever. Pat bellowed, "Keep Leotie in that school, you hear? I'll let you go."

"Great, can't wait to see your speech, bye Dad."

Pat clicked the smart, a sense of calm wrapping around him despite the noise. He could see the living room, P.J. running through it with paper stuck on his head, Leo following and giving him orders and supplying a story—'Going crazy again! He thinks he's a king.—Stand up straighter.—Now he's an anteater. A pug. A cyclone—look out!' Jesse, the good mother, with every other room in the house in perfect order, standing watch. Laird, loosening his tie absently and wrapping his arm around her waist. A family postcard.

Then, as if he'd put the postcard down, he blanked the do-not-disturb and saw his smart had been under fire in the last dozen minutes: fifty-six messages and seventeen calls! His skin got tight. He scanned the smart—it seemed there was a real bomb threat; he scanned the sky, as if he'd see evidence of it—dirty brown clouds were pushing their way out of the Gulf.

"Why do I care about a bomb threat, Tuck?" he raised his voice over the banginge and turned, knowing his lieutenant was lurking near the car.

Tuck was not agile but he was trim and moved decisively, joining Pat quickly and talking loud and fast, "Planted in the Petro Patch. Hydrogen tanks."

Pat scanned back to the junk message about hydrogen bombs—was this nuclear? Plastics? "So?"

"There's a terrorist, he's saying it's personal. It's about you, Guv."

Pat's eyes snapped away from the screen. Tuck wasn't smirking, he was serious. "What?"

Tuck said, "He calls himself the Worm. And he says he can blow up half of Houston."

Pat snorted, "Oh, come on, Tuck."

"Some kind of chain reaction. He blows one hydrogen tank with a bomb, and that gets the next one and the next in a row, and fire could even spread from plant to plant—chain reaction. We're meeting experts and the Guard over at the Corral soon as we get over there."

Pat sensed the earth shifting beneath him and looked down to make sure it was just a sensation and not an earthquake. Closer to his face, the junk message blinked—*Hiroshima...*How had that message pushed through? He'd better check with IT. He focused again at the ground...it wasn't moving...there was a fine layer of dust on his polished shoes. He said automatically, "Let's go." Tuck didn't say 'finally' out loud, but Pat sensed it from his manner.

Pat took deliberate steps as Tuck loped back to the car; the ground remained solid, and that old relish for a challenge bubbled up. "Tuck, what about the mayor?"

Tuck hesitated with his hand on the car door, "Mayor's got police mobilized. Media hasn't heard yet."

"Keep it that way," he ordered. "Don't use the word terrorist. This is home-grown, sounds like. And get feelers out to our Gang. They better invite somebody from the other side." He considered a moment—might as well take on the tiger. "Senator Mack, she's in town."

"MackSucks?" Tuck asked, his face displaying dismay and amazement.

"Senator Mack, you heard me," Pat growled. "What a ruckus," he grumbled escaping into the back seat.

Once settled inside, Pat realized his face and neck were soaked and that the pounding outside was getting louder. He increased the A/C and wiped off with a disposable towel, dusting his shoes clean with the other side of it. As the driver pulled onto the road, he leaned back in the seat and studied the messages. After a minute, he picked up a new call.

"Governor," he said into the smart.

"You picked up."

The voice had a throaty juvenile quality to it, but hard. It seemed to have suddenly muffled all sound. Only the dim hum of the road and the dull blankness of the audio signal.

Pat swallowed and it sounded loud in his ears. "Who's this?"

"Don't you know?"

Baffled, Pat looked at the screen and swallowed, realizing he'd gotten caught unawares again—this guy knew how to hack the Governor of Texas! That *troubled* sensation—he refused to name it *fear*—returned to his midsection.

Trapped, he played gruff: "How'd you get my number?"

"I'm the Worm, Governor Steadson." As if this explained everything.

Though the car was moving, Pat suddenly felt like he'd been halted at the end of a dead-end drive and, stuck, was frantically confirming there was no way out. Who was this guy? His brain shot out suspicions: a scam artist? a political stuntman launched by the dirty liberals? a real terrorist?

Pat mocked, "Worm, huh? I don't talk to Worms."

"I'm from your past, Governor Steadson. I'll call back at eleven. It's time for a reckoning."

Before Pat could reply, a loud pop signaled that the caller had disconnected.

Chapter 2: The Hotel

Tanya dropped her briefcase on the side table in the hotel suite, feeling like a stranger in a haunted house. She chuckled—how many Dem-Reps in history had even been *inside* the Corral Hotel? The room they'd booked for her was on the first floor, looking out at the rear parking lot. Her team was already ensconced and didn't even look up—Feebee on the sectional and Dennis in a soft chair, their faces in their screens. A crazy city emergency, what was a U.S. Senator going to do?

"Anything yet?" Tanya asked without much hope.

Dennis looked up and mentioned innuendo and then recounted some inconsistencies: which plastics plant was the target, was it sabotage, had a bomb actually been planted or would it be rigged later, and was—or wasn't?—lightning the match to light the fuse. Feebee merely shrugged. Tanya said 'okay' and let the younger people probe. She unpacked the briefcase and set up to review the video of the Guv's speech at a work table.

She was thirsty and hungry, but she didn't want to bother with room service or the kitchen. After the laptop booted, and Steadson's face appeared on the screen, she felt her lip curl just like it had when she heard the speech live. This was a problem, she knew, in her political life—the bosses had harped on it when they put the gag order on her last year. Live, the same up-curling lip had come close to peeling off, but fortunately no cameras caught it because she was shorter than the men around—a small advantage. No visible sign of sarcastic disgust captured for posterity. She sighed and pictured tomorrow's headline: *The Hero of Houston Vows, 'I'll do everything I can.'*

Well, got to stay objective. Got to analyze. Got to shoot the speech full of holes and quietly pass along the analysis. Can't stay emotional (masculism). Can't stay pissed (judgement-clouding). Can't make jokes in public, can't speak spontaneously (gag order).

"Damn," she said out loud, because she was pissed and needed to unload some of the piss. "No, Jerk, the sky isn't falling, toxic particulates are falling.—I thought this guy was an economics major. Doesn't he understand real costs? Anyone?" The young people didn't look up. "Hey, who signs your paychecks?" she teased.

"Probably not," Dennis mumbled. Tanya sometimes couldn't believe she had such a genius on her staff—the mind behind Real Time Fact Checker, that might just seriously wound the evil network! His next comment was deflating. "Not sure what we're doing here, Senator."

"I know. We're a resource, maybe." She knew a U.S. Senator had little to do with a state and city emergency, but politics, as Willie always said, never seemed to sleep.

Feebee piped up with, "Senator, I like this one."

Tanya looked at Feebee's feed. A local geek response to the Guv's speech was, 'We're drowning in hubris.' She nodded: "Well okay that's good." However, the pleasurable wave of spite passed almost instantly. "But Feeb, how do we deal with it?" Their eyes met: it was rhetorical, and useless, and soon everyone looked back to their screens.

Did Steadson really *not* care about the future? Was status quo *worth* the end of the world? Were the man and his cronies literally *blind*? And what if he won the nomination and then won the Presidential election, what next? She huffed, the angry tears threatening like the storm that was gathering over the Gulf. No. Can't get that kind of sad-mad. It was partly fear response—the Corral Hotel had old bad associations—lies and cruel stratagems had been conjured here, no doubt, but...

But Steadson would have to care about the present. And Tanya needed to deal with him and the crisis now. He had asked for her, and they had agreed, and the meeting about the terrorist would be soon. No time for wallowing in anger or projecting disaster.

"What about this Worm or whatever—no clue who it is yet?"

Dennis said, "Nuanced. Hard to figure out." He sounded defensive. Tanya could only see his shiny black hair and flickering lenses.

Tanya said more cheerfully than she felt, "Keep at it, Wolf. Don't rush, get it right."

Shit, nobody had given her enough facts. But let the aides do their job. Her job was deal with Steadson. The speech transcription had loaded, so she re-watched and muted the governor's husky voice (and sexy voice, which also pissed her off) and read his words instead. *"If you don't like the energy policies in our state, go elsewhere. There are forty-nine other states in the Union. Plenty of other opportunities. Nobody's stopping you. But we're Texas. We're prospering. And we're going to keep right on prospering. I want to thank—"*

Another Feebee message shot under her glance: *Last Year's Mack Meme Makes Comeback: 'The largest criminal organization in the world might be the Whig Party.'* Tanya smirked—one of many quotes that got her bosses duct-taping her mouth shut. She buzzed her lips, as if the image of tape stopping her mouth had to be broken. Yes, she felt confined everywhere she went—cramped. When she and Loo had been in the D.C. humidity, she had wanted to escape to Houston. Now she was in Houston humidity, inside a creepy hotel, she wanted to escape again, this time to...where? Some*where* far away west...a place in a romance movie....But 'no sex' flashed. It was too early. Romance + no sex = ?

"Been to Hawaii, Feebee?"

Feebee's eyes got big and she shook her head. "California's my west max. Heart San Diego. The beaches...are bliss."

Tanya smiled, "I'd take bliss right now."

Was San Diego humid? Neither she nor Loo liked humidity, Loo certainly wouldn't like it in Hawaii, either. Tanya wondered how Loo's math test had gone. Or was that tomorrow? Will, of course, would have known—how in the world was she supposed to go it alone? She ruminated on this every day. Toughing it out, without Wise Willie, even though it was impossible. Be tough: three hundred sixty days and counting. Getting no easier. Shit, why couldn't she focus on the moment? Drummed her fingers. Dennis' eyes jabbed back and forth but Feebee seemed to be stoned. Sending a personal note?

Tanya gave up on focus and chided, "Feebee." The young woman put down her smart with that touch of guilt that clearly stated, 'Boyfriend'. Tanya continued, "There's got to be a way to get these hard-liners to think long-term. You're young, what do you think?"

"Besides the obvious?" Feebee asked, maybe stalling.

Tanya changed tactics—Feebee wasn't philosophical. "Got to fix this narrative somehow." Feebee gave her a wise look that indicated, 'We could use their tactics.' Tanya forced a fake laugh and shook a finger. "When you're a senator, Feebee, you can try out your scheme."

The young woman shrugged. "Their propaganda machine runs 24/7. Noise on noise. We could get our own network, do the same."

Willie had provoked her along that line, too. "Would you kill for it?" She'd been shocked—no, never! Lie to reverse climate change? Steal if necessary? Maybe. But kill? Something about it hadn't been just an idle question, although Will often asked philosophical or ethical questions and then enjoyed arguing with her. Had he foreseen riots and rolling natural disasters and violence over top of it? How else to break this hard, calcified shell the Whigs and the privileged had built to hold so many dirty secrets?

She scrolled back to the top of Steadson's speech and drafted a list of counterpoints. As the speech restarted, the governor's words read, *"It was right here in Houston that I stood up against the energy crisis. And we overcame the crisis. And we prospered. Now, I'm going to stand up against a new crisis. A crisis of irrational fear."*

Tanya paused the video and wrote a note—'When has he used fear before.' She looked back at the video; Pat Steadson's mouth was open to speak the next sentence, his hand up, his handsome face a bit distorted by rounded lips, wavy hair a tidy blend of brown and grey:

manly, confident, and apparently unaware. Apparently? Tanya shook her head and reminded herself not to feel helpless or surprised. Those were always foolish ways. The phrase 'drowning in hubris' came back. What was hubris, exactly? Dennis would know—but his taut eyebrows indicated he was deep in his search. A bomb crisis short-term: Steadson might excel at coping. The climate crisis long-term: Steadson lagged.

Tanya clicked on Lexicon/Hubris; the definitions brought back old knowledge: *Pride. Overweening pride. Dangerous, deadly, tragic pride.* Tanya was writing the word 'tragic' when she remembered that the tragic hero always has a flaw. What was the chink in Pat Steadson's armor? Not his Whig Party's...but in just him, one man? Was that the way to take them on, through one man's weakness?

'By God,' she thought, 'I'm finally going to be close enough to talk to that man face to face. We've barely bumped into each other for years—hammering each other from a distance. It's a crisis, but we oughta talk, one-on-one. How easy!—let's do it!'

She knew she should get permission and she knew the bomb threat came first, but—'No! Not asking permission. Why? I'm a Senator. Cut through all bullshit. Steadson isn't always irrational. Seventy percent of the time he is. Maybe the crisis will bring out the thirty percent.'

She noticed her palms itching as she sprang out of the hotel chair and declared, "I'm stepping out. Back before the meeting. We'll do a 10-minute huddle, okay, Wolf?" Dennis nodded, eyes hooded. He opened his mouth, closed it. Tanya had spoken while moving toward the door of the suite but she stopped, raised her eyebrows encouragingly and waited. Had he perceived her impulse to go find someone and do something? The mayor, the governor, someone, and talk sense? "I got you."

After a moment, his mouth opened again: "We have a saying. Keeps going through my head. 'Pay attention to the whispers, so we won't have to listen to the screams.'" Tanya felt the force of the words, almost wincing at the notion of screams of agony. She waited for more. Dennis was thoughtful and moved at his own pace, which she had learned to trust. Feebee had gone still on the couch, even though she was looking down at her screen. Dennis' eyes emerged above the screen, his look distant, as if he was gazing over the prairie to predict the weather. "The Worm made things look off the cuff. But it's all been carefully planned, I think, to confuse us. He wants to do something big."

"Big as in destruction?" Tanya asked involuntarily.

"I...don't know. I'm torn by what I see."

"The bomb threat is only part of it?"

"It's like...it's like it's a demonstration."

"What's that?"

"A diversion without direct contact." Dennis shrugged. "I don't know. I smell something big."

Feebee put in, "NOAA says tonight's going to be a killer thunderstorm."

Tanya might have said 'Thanks,' and didn't even grab her purse before she was out the door. The impulse to intervene was supercharging her, and time was against her. She visualized knocking on the Guv's door. She pressed the elevator button up. She would have to guess which floor—the penthouse, probably. She heard murmurs from the distant lobby while she waited. Shit, she used to love Houston, it was home; now she was a stranger in this house worried about screams of agony. What had happened?

Finally, the elevator opened and she hurried inside. Before she could press any button, however, a charming woman sidled in next to her; the doors shut, trapping in a damp summer gardenia odor. The other woman swiped a card and the elevator went up. She seemed lost in thought, mutely off-gassing perfume. When the doors opened again, like a huge exhale, it was on a semi-dark hallway, and the woman glided confidently one way and Tanya, almost gasping for breath and following luck, strode the other way, using her 'D.C.' walk as Will called it.

Soon, she stopped. 'I smell something big,' Dennis had said. But where was it to be found? Tanya had no committee to go to; she was on enemy ground; and she was looking to confront Pat Steadson without a clear plan, and she didn't even know if she was on the right floor! Still, time pressed.

The hallway lights had all been dimmed—it was eerie, as if it were past curfew. She continued down the hall cautiously. A door swung open at the far end and she heard, simultaneously, a toilet flushing. She shouldered into an inset doorway and bumped against a door handle; without thinking, she turned it and it opened and she slipped inside. A heavy tread could be heard and then died away. She looked around—she was in a small room full of cleaning supplies; there was another door opposite. Why was she skulking in a maintenance closet? Why did she feel time was against her and she had to rush?

She tiptoed through the semi-secret place. Gingerly, she opened the other door and found a narrow room with a narrow bed, a single window, and yet another door on the right wall. A maze. She continued softly and tried this door—locked; it must allow access to the adjoining suite, like a 'servant's quarters'...how quaint. Next, she checked the window, flicking open the latch and giving it a push, and in rushed summer heat and inarticulate male voices. So close she could practically touch it, she glimpsed an adjacent terrace and sliding door, drapes; maybe a screen door...the voices emanating from...one sounded like Steadson: shit, it must be the governor's suite! Right there!

"Quality not quantity," floated over.

She couldn't hear the reply but the sounds pulled at her. She judged she could hop across to the terrace and get close enough to eavesdrop and hop back. She considered that, except she was dressed wrong: how could she hoist herself up and through this narrow window in a silk blouse and heels? Was a chance at intelligence worth it? Why not just go out, look around, and knock on Steadson's door and say, 'Let's talk'?

"It's a winner...nah..."

The voices rose and fell as she moved the bed to the window and stood on it. The air smelled dirty-damp and her pores cranked out sweat. She leaned toward the window and her shoe punctured the bed-sheet. Swearing, she adjusted her weight but it was no good—she wobbled and couldn't even get her head stuck out before she lost her balance, one leg twisting as a snapping noise caused her to retreat and sit down on the bed. A heel had broken off. She grabbed the other shoe and wedged it against the bed frame and wrenched at it to make the shoes even. They were Italian, she recalled, as she strained until the heel broke. Sweating everywhere now, she peeled off her suit jacket.

What am I doing? part of her brain argued. Hear what? Party secrets of the foe? The foe who was kicking them day after day, election after election? Another part imagined herself as a spy—not a hard-core spy from a tough spy novel—a spy from a romantic thriller, finding out the true connection between the bomber and Steadson.

Well, she was now in 'flats', and waded in half-way, so she stood again and stuck her head out the window. The voices were still audible. She was petite enough, she judged, to squeeze through. So she pushed forward, using her hips to perch on the sill. The adjacent terrace, sheltered from the murky brown sunlight, was fairly dark; through a screen door the sliding glass looked half open; beyond, drapes revealed only shadows. She listened a few moments, hearing a clinking sound, and then a howl, a brief guffaw, and deep talk—vowels, almost no consonants, too muffled to make sense.

Balancing on her side, she saw that the hotel architect had no thought of designing it so someone could navigate this window ledge and skip easily across to the adjacent terrace. But the faux stucco facade was punctuated by generous thick concrete moldings extending several feet beyond the frame of every window. God, she thought, this is stupid—I haven't attempted gymnastics since high school. She wriggled her knees up and crouched. Her body had done all manner of strange choreography with that aerial dance troupe the summer after college, which she'd forgotten, but she trusted her body had remembered a few things and her balance felt good. 'I work out every day,' she reminded herself.

Emboldened, she raised up on the ledge and eased forward past the extent of the window to the edge of the thick border, her arms automatically assuming second position and, without pausing, took a long stride-hop over the gap and tapped onto the railing, which she could scarcely believe was so easy, though this moment of self-consciousness led to an immediate loss of kinesthetic awareness and she went to her knees, rocking on the rail and flailing her hands down to grab hold to regain balance, which worked fine, and she steadied, and then overbalanced and had to collapse as she swung sideways, still clinging to the rail so her body lowered-sprawled onto the concrete—thunk...better than swinging the other way twelve floors down to the courtyard pavement and splat.

"Yep," smacked out Steadson's voice.

She was afraid she'd been seen. But maybe when they talked sometimes they were turned toward the door. Her side, shoulder and cheek became acquainted with the concrete, some dust, and a few dried leaves. As she drew panting breaths she thought it should have hurt more, but she had landed on the fatty part of her butt like you're supposed to, not on a bone. Lying there, an awkward former-dancer-gymnast-now-senator and spy, she almost laughed aloud at herself. She half-expected a choreographer's critique when her eye caught fuzzy sight of patent leather shoes just yards away, glimpsed through a screen and beneath the drapes' ends. She drew a sharp breath.

A moment later, a harsh voice rang out clearly, "Idiots. Unbelievable."

She tensed up, alarmed she was so close, because what if they came out on the terrace? How in the world could she ever explain what she was doing here? She was scared and thrilled all at once—her career could end. Or, she could learn something to take down these hard-asses. Like: what if this Worm terrorist was their plot?

"What does?" Steadson's familiar husky voice interrupted her disorganized thoughts. "I said what does?"

"Selfishness." A burst laugh. Who was this guy?

"And keeps us together?" It must be Guv's shoes she could see. Nice shoes, she liked a man with—

"No, that's common interests," the other man said.

"Get to the point, I don't got time for double-talk."

"Come on now, don't get pious, we got people handling that. All I'm saying is I need you solid." She wished she were recording! She'd left her device in her purse! Was it Steadson's handler giving him political directives? Campaign angles?

"I never endorsed it."

"Now it's different."

"Never will."

"Come on, Pat, we stay together." She felt herself shaking her head—it seemed hard to believe anyone could make arrogant Pat Steadson do anything. "Done deal."

"You sure? I'll put state election offices on notice."

"Why?"

"And fund it. I got money in the budget for rural counties."

"Goddammit!" The shoes moved away, and Tanya relaxed. But shifting her gaze, she had to suppress the urge to yelp when she saw hairy legs—a spider was crawling under her nose; this close, it looked enormous. She shuddered but stayed put; the spider stopped; then it scuttled out of sight. She squeezed her eyes shut. Why was she so afraid of a little spider?

The other man's voice got louder. "I don't get you. This from you. Gerry king. Look, all we're doing is limiting the days—nothing illegal. It's working just fine in Florida."

"Florida!", the governor sounded derisive. "This is my State. We play loose sometimes but we play fair!"

Tanya almost snorted—talk about hypocrisy, re-drawing voting district borders was okay, but he was against outright voter suppression? Then again, for all his faults, the Guv didn't strike her as a cheater. And randomly, hadn't his wife been bi-racial?

"Pat," the man cooed, "Don't lose your temper. Just leave it, okay? The models work fine. We'll take care of it."

"I keep telling you people, tactics come back to bite. All you think about is short gain. Never cost."

"Don't tell me my job," the other man warned. "I win us seats, every year, that's what I do."

"Burnin' bridges s'okay long as you're willing to rebuild," Steadson drawled, sounding more Texian. "Problem with you is never doin' the rebuild. Heck, all you know how to do is scare people from crossin' the stream. You're Zero Sum, and I'm not, okay?"

Tanya felt a glimmer of hope—the Guv wasn't a scarcity fanatic, he was an optimist!

The rebuff came quickly, "Goddammit don't fight me on this, Pat. That's the business we're in."

"Don't tell me how to do business. You're talkin' coward business. I don't do that kinda business."

"Everybody stays in line!"

"Well. Count me out of line and outta lies." Steadson's voice was exultant.

Tanya's neck felt stiff and she allowed herself to adjust, sweeping the area quickly with her eyes to check for spiders. Then the drapes swung and she saw a pale hand hovering in the air! It must be on Steadson's shoulder—yes, that was a dark blue suit—next to Steadson's thick hair. "Let's work this out. Come out, get some fresh air."

Tanya's body stretched in opposite directions, wanting to curl up in a ball and stand up with her hands on her hips defiantly at the same time. She did neither—she froze. The screen door grated open a few inches and then grated shut while Steadson said something—his shoes were practically next to her toes, separated only by a screen door!

The other man was saying in a soothing tone, "You got a big job in a big state. And big things comin maybe."

"What I got's a crisis. We're done here, I told you what I'm doin."

"You're gonna need me, goddammit."

"Way I see it, maybe you need me, but I don't need you. I sure don't need you for me to do the right thing."

At that, the drapes twitched, the slider clanged shut, the shoes vanished. A few moments later a slamming sounded followed by breaking glass. Tanya pressed herself beside a plastic planter in the darkest part of the corner. More glass—was it murder? a brawl?

Be tough, fight if she had to. Timid around violence, she flinched away from hurting people, she'd been in one scrape with a bigger girl in grade-school and after one swing got chopped to the ground and ate gravel. Still, she could defend herself. Maybe it wasn't glass but a gun shot, or maybe they were throwing glasses. No yelling. There would be police if it had been a gun, right? Police would come out here and look around...would her career end just to learn Steadson wasn't as bad at voter suppression as his handler? Would her body be found beneath this planter, in her broken shoes?

Like before, she acted decisively on instinct, unfreezing and, without looking back, escaped: she gained the rail, hoisted herself up. Bending and springing—up higher this time—she landed back on the molding, tight-roping it to the window and grabbing the sill. She felt the urge to look down; instead, clutching the open window frame, feeling the A/C cool inside on one hand while the other sweated in the humid heat, she glanced at the skyline of Houston and puffy clouds on the horizon. She wanted to be in a sudsy bathtub...or in a silk robe in bed, reading, with...with a good man in her lap. Her imagination wasn't very helpful sometimes, she thought, and ducked her head and squeezed back through the window.

The **Worm** was uncomfortable. He chafed and puffed in the wheelchair, inflating the lumbar support a bit more, easing the seat tilt a few millimeters, knowing all of it was just a distraction. His body would remind him that a slightly different discomfort provided only the illusion of respite. He'd already dosed so there was nothing to be done...unless—he thought not for the first time—he became a heroin addict and eased the misery as much as he wanted. He consciously deflected the pain signals and closed his eyes. His face felt like it was smoothing out—like it had been all twisted and now crisped flat, like a fresh sheet of butcher paper.

As so often, he re-lived the face floating over him and his astonishment that the pounding—which should have stopped—didn't. And as he drifted away, with the pain both becoming more acute and yet remote, the rewind went...walking over to pick up the stick. It was his nature, he concluded bitterly: fight, not flight.

Pat was reviewing the briefing notes, getting ready to answer the tricky questions. (Like wasn't this a good reason to invest in green energy?) There was an energetic buzz in the room as two hundred people crowded in.

"Here the turkeys come," Tuck muttered, slipping in his usual distaste of the media. "Can't we send them to Mars, Guv?"

He deflected this attempt at humor. "No air on Mars."

Tuck was frowning, jabbing the air with his finger. "Wouldn't be a bad idea." Pat grunted, hoping he'd shut up and get the briefing organized. "Look at 'em circle."

"Tuck." The practiced tone blending exasperation and command in equal measure shut up his lieutenant. Pat felt an inward head-shake; it was a serious crisis; why was the guy so unhelpful? Was he angry that he didn't get to be on TV? In his sleek new suit? Pat rattled off some orders: "Go get that briefing room organized and ready. I make a quick statement to media—I don't need you for that. Before the meet up, I want fifteen minutes. Make sure I'm not disturbed. Right?"

Tuck shrugged, Pat glared, and so Tuck turned and fought his way through the massed reporters. A few minutes later, Pat surveyed the room and broadly waved an arm over his head and boomed, "Ladies and Gentlemen!" The camera people scrambled. Keep it informal, don't go to the lectern. Being tall was an advantage at times like this. "Could you all please wait until after my briefing and I'll make a statement. Give us an hour plus, okay?" A smart rang and was silenced. Smoothly, he continued, "You can stay here or go get a bite in the lobby but it'll be an hour at least, not more than two. We'll let you know the time we get close. Now excuse me—emergency State business. Thank you."

He put up a thumb and then hurriedly knifed through the crowd to his suite room door. Open, closed, escaped. He clicked on the dining table light. The broken glass was gone; vacuum streaks showed on the plush carpet. He picked a hard chair, sat, and resumed skimming the notes. The scale of Houston's industrial complexes was hard to grasp; even the Mayor's report expressed surprise at the amount of damage that could be done by a single 'terrorist'. Cracking polymers was a strange thing. Apparently, it only took one nutcase to turn the process into a massive explosive charge.

Houston. Flat, sprawled out in a flail, a floodplain practically floating in the Gulf. His eye jumped to the water details: 'Sea-level rise'—the names these people came up with for every potential disaster! Hard to remember how to pronounce the water expert's last name. 'Forever chemicals.' A knock, he answered, Tuck looked in, self-Importance cutting into Pat's fifteen precious minutes!

"They're ready any time."

Pat nodded. "What's the water guy's name?"

"Hydrology," Tuck said.

"Yep, hydrology."

"Dick Kenz."

"Like 'pens', correct?"

"Yes, Kenz, like Barbie's twin boyfriends." Pat made a note on his notes. Tuck was elaborating, "Don't forget, he's a Jules guy, who knows how creative he is."

Annoyed, Pat clicked his ballpoint off and on. When had he stopped liking Tuck...? Sometime during the last election; maybe the man's marriage was in trouble? Tuck thought he knew how to fix everything, but he never wanted to take all the steps; he knew how to blame but not how to think strategically. Tuck was not going to like it when the Party told him he wasn't vice presidential material. And probably blame Pat.

Tuck may not, but Pat respected Mayor Desayuno. Disagreed with his politics but knew his ability to work with people, and with a terrorist threat he'd need to: fire and police, the army guard, the scientists, the Feds, the bomb people, PR, finance, you name it. What a wild afternoon and now evening. He and the mayor had to come up with a plan quick and promise the world they'd get rid of this 'evil' in Houston. Because if the Worm did what he promised...Pat looked back at his notes. 'Any chain of explosions will be devastating.' Everybody loved to exaggerate. Was Kenz right about the potential scale of this disaster? Pat reviewed the bullet points and shook his head. Why did people build cities on floodplains? The image of cereal floating in milk came to mind. He realized he was hungry and that Tuck was fiddling with his smart.

Before he could tell him to get out, Tuck cried, "Holy fuck, I think it's the nut—ON MY LINE!"

Pat held out his hand—Tuck was irresolute—Pat snapped his fingers and took Tuck's smart and answered, "Governor."

The juvenile voice was sulky. "Careful what you say in public, Hero, or I'll end the game. Have your briefing. No mass evacuations. No deployments. No infiltrations. No power outages. Anything like that, game over. Follow my instructions. Only way to keep Houston safe."

The connection dropped and Pat clenched his teeth so he wouldn't swear out loud.

Tanya was a little out of breath as she exited the maintenance closet, her gait wobbly thanks to the nubs where the shoe heels had been. She was proud of her restoration of suit jacket to cover the blouse stains, water to clean off the concrete dust and dirt on the pants. A clean face towel and a few cosmetic supplies in the narrow room had been an unlooked-for boon. According to the tiny mirror, her hair and makeup looked like one might expect it at the end of a busy work day. She just had to manage the shoes and keep her lip curling when she confronted Steadson.

She did her D.C. stride into the hall, pressing the balls of her feet harder forward to reduce the sideways tilt. Staffers and a few media people were milling around like men outside church on Sunday, and no one seemed to notice her appearance or its origin. She saw Mayor Desayuno and nodded; he acknowledged her but was busy with a cluster of people. She took a deep breath and shouldered through a knot of suits until she reached Steadson's suite. As she raised a hand to knock a nasal voice chided,

"Ah-ah, not unless I say so."

It was the Lieutenant Governor, the shiny hard-liner. They had never met. Oh, but she knew secrets about him. How did these people keep getting worse? No wonder his wife was filing for divorce. What was her name—Donna? Don and Donna?

"Excuse me, sir, but Mayor Desayuno—"

"No let me repeat, no one gets in there unless I say so. The Governor is not to be disturbed." He wedged between her and the door, elbowing her breast in the process and bumping her back a step. Then he leaned against the door, arms folded. The hubbub in the hall continued, seeming to say, 'You're on our turf, not the Mayor's.'

Volcanic fury bubbled up inside Tanya's breast. Not only had the man banged her in the boob but he hadn't shown her any form of respect—not her name or 'ma'am' or senator. Or maybe it was partly from the adrenaline still in her system from the spying ordeal—just survived one mission in enemy territory only to fight in another. She looked him over: strong-featured but not handsome; his eyes icy hazel; thin lips; purposely devoid of social grace. How best to play him? She led with politeness.

"Lieutenant Governor Knobs, we haven't met, I'm Senator Mack."

"Oh I know who you are," he said.

'Prick', she thought. "Mayor Desayuno," she lied, "Gave me permission to speak to the governor before the meeting. Please tell him Senator Mack is here."

"And why should I do that for your boy Jules?"

"Because it's your job," she said. She sensed her own constricted breathing. She turned her head sideways and bit her tongue so she wouldn't call him 'asshole', the word hovering in her mouth like a bad taste.

"It's also my job," he began with a half-smile that warned her he was about to say something unpleasant, "To protect my people and keep them secure."

"From what?"

"Oh little things like distractions or big things like executions," he drawled. Her stomach jerked—was he insinuating she or her cohort had called in the bizarre confession/execution on the majority whip? Knobs' sudden attack was telling: he wasn't afraid to say anything as long as it was antagonistic! Off-kilter webcam footage of the half-naked, trussed-up opponent she'd secretly called 'Walrus' jumped into her mind. She looked at this new bully—he was too crude to get too far, right? He pressed on, "Anyway, don't you realize we're in a crisis, so the governor's time is, shall we say, curtailed? I can't let in every blubbering woman who knocks on the door."

A year ago, Tanya would have kneed this prick in the prick. Before weeping uncontrollably at Will's funeral became a national joke and men like Knobs brought it up at every town hall or rally. Before the bosses laid down the etiquette: 'Control your emotions, Senator, avoid confrontations and keep your mouth shut.'

But tonight the crisis had broken open the bars and she was on the hunt. "Mr. Knobs," she said heatedly, still considering a knee to the groin, "You are a servant of the public obstructing me from doing her job. Haven't you got anything to offer besides obstruction?" The man just smirked. "And blame, of course." The smirk vanished, and she relaxed her leg. No need to knee this bastard. She played another card: "I wonder what the governor would say if I told him you were planning to run against him in the next Presidential election." Knobs' eyes got icier. "I doubt you are ready for that information to reach his ears." She sensed the lever return to her hands and she leaned on it: "Now, in order for me to keep that to myself, and believe me I would prefer to do that for my own reasons, I expect you to treat me respectfully. You will address me as Mrs. Mack or Senator Mack." She raised her eyebrows as a prompt. Knobs' face looked frozen but his hands were vibrating. "Try it."

"Senator Mack."

"Want to apologize for your sexist remark next?"

"What remark?"

"Mr. Knobs, some day you may have more power than I do. But not today. I'm a U.S. Senator." She noted him reading the sub-textual message, 'And you are a glorified secretary.' She watched his face twist into a sort of half-sneer. She said forcefully, "You will apologize for pretending you didn't know you had made a sexist remark *and* for your sexist remark."

He stared, as if to test her, then his eyes dropped. Somewhat robotically, his body hitched straighter and he said, "I apologize for my insensitive joke, Senator Mack."

"Thank you, Mr. Knobs, but that's not good enough. 'Blubbering Woman' is not insensitive. And not a joke. Not to mention that blubbering means weeping and I wasn't weeping. So, inaccurate. And, sexist."

Without prompting, he parroted, "I apologize for my remark which, I can see, could be taken as sexist and was not...accurate."

"You will also apologize for insinuating that I am a criminal capable of ordering an act of cruelty and murder."

His Adam's apple bounced and he said mechanically but faintly, "I apologize. Senator Mack."

She debated following up with a vindictive 'thank you', which would feel good, but she decided he was beat up enough for one day. "Now, as I said, Mayor Julio Desayuno is helping the governor during this crisis. Please tell the Governor that Senator Mack is here to see him."

Again, like a robot or, she reconsidered, a zombie, he rapped on the door, entered, murmured something, and held the door open for her and then closed it behind her. She was inside Steadson's suite—a crude enemy behind, a crafty enemy in front!

She suppressed a giggle over her victory and immediately felt a flash of anxiety. She cleared her throat and looked around—the penthouse suite was predictably large and lavish. It had a dead fireplace fronted by two cushy chairs, a long glittering bar, a wide hallway—with an outline which must lead to the 'servant's quarters'—opening up on a spacious Italianate bathroom. A vast kitchenette with an island was nearby, where a light clicked off and a figure emerged from the shadows.

Tanya stood face to face with the media-dubbed, 'Traitor of Texas', Pat Steadson. In a quieter version of the husky-easy voice she had heard earlier at the podium (and again while crouching on the terrace beyond the sliding door), he welcomed her: "Evening, Senator, I've only got about five minutes."

Involuntarily, she glanced at his shiny leather shoes. She remembered his overheard remark denying the winners and losers mentality of his Party Boss. The hope she felt crouching on the terrace came back, and she looked up into his steady eyes and said, "Thank you for seeing me, Governor, let's talk."

The **Worm** visualized his henchfolk. Most were unwitting of course, because that way they couldn't change their minds. Except for H.E. No, the others were just doing things he'd 'programmed' them to do in advance. Kind of like the way genes program bodies. But like a gene, the Worm had no power over what the bodies actually did with the programming. He couldn't contact them—his positive reinforcement was purely mental. The routine was in motion, and the Worm was out of contact. Still, he sent them good will.

He felt a pain in his lower back. Checked the time—three hours. Things to do. He wheeled through the empty server room, humming off-key, 'There Goes the Chief'.

Pat was fatigued. It was eight o'clock, he hadn't eaten since breakfast, he'd cleared the way to become a candidate for president, he'd been on national television once already and would be again, his beloved granddaughter was miserable, his deputy was a jerk, the Party handler was mad at him, and every few seconds his brain shook him up with the question: Who could The Worm be? The emergency had turned everything inside out.

The staff culling info from the web reported, 'It's personal, among all the memes, it's personal.' Meanwhile, a dem-rep senator had forced her way into his suite, offering help while simultaneously raging about the safety of her daughter. Frankly, he couldn't blame her, but wasn't it over the top?

"Senator, would you please sit down?" he asked irritably.

But no, she preferred walking back and forth gesticulating and advising him to think *ethically*. He had never spoken to Mack at any length. He'd been briefed about her, but when she surprised the country by winning one of Texas' U.S. Senate seats he had asked for a more productive analysis. She was shorter than he would've thought and younger, what, maybe early forties? Actual age didn't matter, she seemed forty-ish. The Latinos liked her—she talked their language. A loud-mouth at first but lately not so much. Frankly, he did sizing up people in person, and he felt eager despite the chaos of the hour.

A little breathless pacing back and forth, her voice was pleasant but she could drive points forcefully. Poised and fluid...and something else: she cared. He saw her love and concern for children, hers and everyone's, and he thought of Leo.

He was glad he had chosen Mack to communicate with the other side—she had a personal stake in it, she lived in Houston, she had a daughter. Good. That was something to justify giving her some time right now. Next, how to play ball with her. Five minutes would go fast. He considered popping her philosophical balloon, but something told him not to be aggressive.

She had paused in her portrayal of the crisis and he drawled softly, "Senator, I do appreciate your interest, but would you please—"

"Mr. Steadson, stop asking me to sit down. I am not going to sit down. I said 'no' already. When I say 'no', what do you think I mean?"

He felt abashed. Certain women, he realized, could do this to him—women who had won his respect. "Fair enough. I apologize. You keep saying 'ethics'. Please, tell me in plain English how you can help me with this crisis."

This brought her to a halt. She had gone perfectly still as she looked at him and said in a clear voice, "I can help you *if*. *If* I get you to about the helpless. Children. The under-privileged. Mother Earth. I certainly don't want the biggest ecological disaster in American history to go down right under my nose in my hometown. You hear me?"

She stood almost straight-on, head slightly tilted up to look him in the face, her expression demanding an answer. Forceful and clear, yes, and with heart. The concerned parent...more useful than the 'Green Freak'.

He stopped short of nodding in agreement. "Please, Senator..." he almost asked her to sit down again. To cover his near-mishap, he started toward the kitchen. "Coffee? Soda pop? Alcohol?" She shook her head. "Watermelon?"

"Oh." As if it was a guilty secret, she muttered, "I love watermelon."

"Me too. I like to eat before a briefing, don't you?"

She nodded. "Watermelon, my husband's favorite."

He glanced at her, but she seemed lost in her memories, looking out the window. He recognized the tone for the loved one, gone. Wait, was she manipulating him? He felt the urge to touch her shoulder. No. Back to business—he opened the refrigerator and got out the pre-cut watermelon. "Where do you guess...?" He opened drawers looking for silverware but could only find one plastic fork.

"Isn't there a real fork?" she asked, missing his meaning. "And a real plate?"

Irritating. Why did everything turn into an eco-war? Plates were easy but he couldn't find any silverware. After opening all the drawers, he heard a thud and a metallic clattering.

"Here," she said, holding up two stainless steel forks.

"Where did you...? Not in the oven?"

"Cupboard." He made face and she shrugged, "Don't ask me why, it's not my...hotel."

Ah, he thought, she's got some humor. He grinned, "You think it's safe?"

She smiled. "Isn't this bi-partisan watermelon?"

"Yep, and I'm sure it'll be tasty."

They ate standing in the kitchen. He replaced Mack with Marta, enjoying a presence at a meal, even a snack. He reminded himself Mack was likely probing him for weakness and that time had stretched beyond five minutes. He let it, he had to, his gut told him it was okay, he was working, this was work, too. He noticed Mack had taken off her shoes, maybe when they were searching for the silverware—what did that mean? His guard came up—was she going to seduce him? She wasn't that type of—he dropped the fork and suddenly felt clumsy.

To cover his embarrassment, he washed off the fork and asked, "You ride horses, Senator?"

"No, Governor. Do you?"

"Sure do. I was just thinking that I used to have a pony that would've suited you."

"A midget horse?"

"Come on, a pony. First horse we got my son, Laird. Sorry, you must get tired of references to your stature."

"Don't you? Airplanes must be no fun." She paused and he had to nod, though it had been a long time since he had flown coach and begged for a bulkhead seat. "What do you get tired of?"

"Oh...well..." Be on guard, he reminded himself, things were better now but a year ago Mack was Enemy #1. She might be an ally during this crisis, *maybe*...but....

But oh it was tempting to retreat into the pleasures of the domestic and feminine world, away from the tiring habit of keeping his guard up, of The Worm and the alleged bomb and the pell-mell city outside and the bunkered plush hotel suite. He missed Marta—she had made such a retreat for them. He checked his watch—in a few minutes, the mayor and police and FBI and Technical and Water and Air and advisors and all the rest of them would look to him to take the lead. And, a fear-mongering part of his brain reminded him that his political life might be over.

"Don't you get tired of all the negatives?" she persisted, probably sucking him in.

"I suppose. Got good support people, though. I stay focused on the big picture." He thought that was generic enough. He gave in to temptation and asked, "You have a daughter, you said? How old?"

"Six."

"Like that age. That's when my granddaughter and I really got close." He wanted to rest and put up his feet and stop fighting and...he looked at her. What did she think of him when she came in—'The Oil Slick'? Had anything changed since? She was looking at him and he thought: Man and woman, tall and short, conservative and liberal. The world is the world is this and that...it all spun around. He hated that, that divide, that endless conflict. He remembered his mentor had said, 'Don't kill yourself trying to understand them. Understand yourself.' Was that good advice? If they sat together a while, would he come to understand her? The idea Marta had that everything was a spectrum, everything—sexuality, love, identity, race, violence, politics—haunted him, wore on him.

This woman with no shoes on in his suite was sexy. An alarm bell rang inside and he quelled a rising urge he felt a twinge of regret

"Well, thanks for stopping by, Senator," he said with finality to protect himself. Best to charge on briskly, "I'd appreciate your keeping a level head through all this. We'll see what you can do to help after the briefing—I'll send someone down personally to your suite."

"You could let me sit in," she suggested.

Ah, that was well-played! He smiled faintly. "*After* the briefing I'll let you know if the Mayor or I can use your help."

"It's a golden opportunity," she offered, leaving her meaning open-ended.

Brisker: "I have a duty to the people of our State, and that duty means I have to go now."

She nodded, disappointment in the roving eyes, but her shoulders were back and her head erect even as she crouched to put on her shoes. She strode resolutely to the door and he followed, intending to open it for her, when she whirled forcing him to withdrew a step. He had seen that dangerous look before on an adversary's face. He braced himself, his heart pumping faster; he didn't have time for another skirmish, she must know that, she must be reasonable! As the seconds dragged, he prepared to say, "Don't," but the energy surging between them choked his breath. He braced himself for her next move.

Tanya inhaled and exhaled without speaking. She couldn't leave without punishing him, but she felt torn. She clenched her fist and told herself to be strong..."Now, before I go, I want to tell you, Mr. Steadson..." She locked eyes with his. "I think the speech you gave today was immoral. Call yourself a Christian, you should know better. What will you tell your granddaughter? That she'll inherit a world where industry got fat until the plankton and shell-making organisms died off and the aquatic food chain collapsed? A world where there aren't enough pollinators and people eat fake food? Where wild fires rage in the west and floods and hurricanes ravage the south? Don't you remember the HURRICANE? Your platform is a slap in our Lord's face. Because it's immoral." And she added softly, "And I know you're not a coward. Listen: keep your granddaughter in mind when you make your next justification. Good night."

However, she was saying all this inside, not outside! She was fantasizing that he would shout at her in reply so she could call him delusional, at which he'd call her names, and she'd play the race card and then there'd be a face-to-face confrontation and, out of nowhere, they'd throw it all up in the air and grab each other and put their mouths together and she'd dig both hands into his thick hair while he eased his big hands to cup her buttocks and lift her against the door and their friction would...! The fantasy would be sexier if she'd worn a skirt and nylons—and she could do without his red tie. But, no matter, the first round would be fierce and quick, followed by a lingering cuddle in the king until she mounted for a slow one...together they might straddle and conquer the great divide!

However, this was no time for fantasies. She chided herself for making up romance plots during a crisis—she betrayed Willie and her constituents and herself. She might have been sweating—had he seen any of these wild thoughts on her face or in her body? What was wrong with her?

When she checked, however, Steadson just looked tired.

She drew herself up and let the wild urges settle. She pointed a steady finger at him. "Every decision we make—EVERY decision—every promise...let's remember our children and grandchildren." Her vision seemed to blur after she'd spoken. "Don't be a coward, please."

He shifted, probably to open the door for her, then seemed to change his mind. "Thank you for the chat, Senator," she heard him saying but she was grasping and pressing the handle and pushing open the door. The sexual was strangled by anger at herself for losing her way at a crucial political moment: feeling empathy for the enemy, and only throwing a weak desperate plea from the heart at the end, instead of grabbing him by the throat.

Thankfully, Steadson's lackey was not around and she hurried past the litter of reporters and security. Her body smelled unpleasant; she yearned for a shower. As she approached the elevator bank, Mayor Desayuno appeared across the hall, coming out of a rest room, looking anguished. When he saw her, she enjoyed that he smiled broadly, and he graciously thanked her and said he was glad she was here. She wanted to be courteous, but she was too wound up.

"Thanks, the Governor is shutting me out of the briefing," she complained bitterly. "So I'll be in my suite, waiting." She pushed the elevator button and doors opened, and before the mayor could offer apologies, she waved escaped. When the doors opened on the first floor, she took off the broken shoes and padded toward her room.

Whoa, she thought, watermelon-ing with Pat Steadson! His face floated before her, as if beckoning her to return: eyes hungry but myopic; brow full but puzzled; gaze firm but tired. She shook away the vision—that face wasn't going to save the state or the country, none of these bastards were, it was going to be a mess! And no, the face wasn't going to make love to her, by God, even though her crazy body had conjured up other ideas and now ached—she giggled to herself at how just fucking *animal* things could get. Willie had never found politics sexy, but there was something....Her door wouldn't open. She fumbled for the key card and the door chimed and swung wide and she giggled again—guess I'm done being angry at myself, she thought, what a ride I just took!

Dennis and Feebee looked up from their screens, plunging her back into the dread of the crisis. Dozens of questions erupted in her mind—would her people have any answers?

She longed to take a shower but instead dropped her shoes and ordered a full report.

After the first round of briefs, **Pat** grouped the staff and assigned tasks. While people clustered, he remembered the curve of Senator Mack's upper lip. When had he last been aroused by a woman? He deliberately wadded up this thought like paper and chucked it away and told the group to hurry up. His first question to the FBI man Miller was if they had checked up on the reporter the Worm had called.

"He's cleared," the man said decisively, shaking his head. "Nothing there."

"How does this Worm guy operate? You don't know and nobody knows who he is or where he is?!!"

"Could we talk privately about this situation, Governor, while your groups meet?"

Steadson scanned the conference room's Party people, aides, his AP, security, national guard, CIA, police chief, fire chief, a lawyer and his entourage huddled together in twos, threes and fours, many talking at once.

He nodded at Miller. "Come into my suite," he said quietly and then beckoned to Tuck, who hurried over. "Tuck, just have to get something straight, tell everybody I want break-outs in fifteen minutes. Keep us on task, okay?"

Tuck nodded and Pat led the guy into his room. The smell of watermelon was gone and with it the senator's vivacity...he didn't want to think of it as sexual energy. Patiently, once again he folded the woman up and dropped her from his thoughts, gesturing to the comfy chairs. The FBI guy took one, he took another.

"What's your name again, please?"

"Special Agent in Charge Miller."

Pat looked him over: short, freckled, dark hair combed flat. A little bit like some creature but not furtive, but the features reminded him of...a river otter. Not a bad association, considering he was FBI. Pat rubbed his temples, hoping to subdue a headache. "Let's get to it, Miller."

"Do you remember a boy in your elementary school named Jon Camel?"

"Jon Camel," the words jerked out of his mouth followed by a clawing in his gut. Immediately he was looking down a tube into the bloody face, head quivering like jelly each time he pounded it, down and down and down. He could feel pound-pounding in his own temples and needles in his midsection. He focused on the panorama of his hotel room again, and on this spy guy...where was this going? Miller wasn't looking directly at him but Pat could feel him gauging his reaction. He crossed his arms and said calmly, "I remember a kid with that name."

"Ah, well, sir." Now the guy stared straight at him. "We think the bomber is him."

Pat blinked, mind fuzzy. "Why..." He was stammering. "Why-why is that?"

"Well, Governor...ahhh..." The FBI man checked his padlet. "We think the 'Worm' is Camel because there are some threads out there that blame you as the cause of the city's trouble, ahh, because you never paid for what you did to him."

Steadson exploded. "Never paid? I never paid!!??" He popped out of the chair and scarcely restrained himself from pounding the counter. "That chicken kid beat me with a stick! I was provoked to say the least! Recess, be-because he wanted the baseball diamond, but it was ours! We were already playing, game in-progress! But no, he comes with his gang across the school-yard to kick our grade out. I don't budge so he whacks me with a big ol' stick, so I punch him. And then, afterwards, my parents insisted we move the hell out of there, which was fine with me. You ever been to Jasper?"

"No sir."

"Well it's hell on earth!" He paused. He realized he'd been shouting. He sat down. He didn't apologize. Miller didn't seem fazed. Quietly, "Ever *heard* of Jasper, Miller?"

"Oh yes I've heard of it."

Pat shivered; who was this guy? The uncertainty ruffled him. He didn't know why he should get so flustered—they were both just doing their jobs. Surely the FBI had sent their best. Miller was waiting patiently, padlet poised on his lap, a device filled with stories from the past. "Sh..." Pat barely stopped himself from swearing.

The muffled talks in the next room inserted themselves into the space that followed. Pat realized how frazzled he was. He got like this after an adrenaline high in front of media knowing it was broadcast to hundreds of thousands. There was always a low, and he still had another rollercoaster ride coming up. He put his hands under his arms—his hands had turned icy—and sat back deliberately in his chair and forced himself to be comfortable.

He adopted a civil, friendly tone. "Special Agent Miller, let me tell you something. After that kid attacked me, I had to start over at a new school in a new town. The fifth one since I started elementary school. I lost all my friends. I hated Jasper, and...well, in hindsight, it was a good move. For one thing, I never had to go to another bad public school." He paused again, realizing this was not very tactful. Too late—

"Public schools were all right for me," Miller said mildly, his eyes soft but steady. Miller was a plain name, but the man's air suggested he was deep.

"Sure, they're not all bad, but some are." What was wrong? Denigrating was not his usual tack, even in back rooms with the back room people. Stay above it. Stay focused. "Anyway. Anyway, whoever it is, the guy must be nuts."

"Well, Governor, excuse me, I don't follow. Paralyzing someone 'cause he hit you with a stick seems excessive to me."

"Paralyzed?" It was as if a hammer had dropped on the top of Pat's head. His eyes were suddenly dry and he blinked over and over. "Paralyzed?"

"You didn't know?"

"Know?"

"Oh." The FBI man seemed a bit puzzled. Then, his training must have kicked in because he went on briskly, "Jon Camel was paralyzed as a result of the beating he received from you."

"That's darn well not true!"

"The medical records show—"

"He was fine, I saw him walking around—"

"The medical records show—"

"His father practically paraded him down Main Street—"

"Governor—"

"They never filed charges!"

"Sir—"

"Never!"

"Sir, please let me finish." Steadson felt the urge to finish *him* with a punch in the mouth. What the hell was going on tonight? It was like everyone was coming after him and he couldn't figure out why or what to do. He swung his hand in the air and demanded the guy talk. Miller said, "The medical records show that Mr. Camel's initial recovery was followed almost immediately by severe complications. He was deemed...diagnosed, pardon me, a paraplegic due to a spinal cord injury."

"I don't believe it. I never heard a word about it. Why wouldn't I have heard about it?"

Miller's mouth went into a line. "Looks like Mr. Camel's family was compensated."

Pat almost swore. "Holy...you mean paid off."

"Our intel says so."

"By who? Who paid? Who...?" But Pat's bewilderment only lasted a few seconds. He knew in a flash and he held up a hand to spare Miller any more. He rubbed his eyes, more tired than ever. "By God, Miller. Let me collect my thoughts." He got up. Yep, he saw it all. Of course Uncle Ted did it. That strange day, unforgettable, when he and the other men showed up for dessert. Like a mobster induction, he always thought it had been. Except no guns, no overt oaths, just smiles and nods and atta-boys. Uncle Ted, winking. But not telling him anything specific.

Poor paralyzed Jon Camel.

If this got out...good bye Presidency. Maybe good bye career. Good bye anything worth doing.

Pat's thoughts came back to the moment. How high was Miller's clearance? The guy was sitting stoic in the chair, looking at his padlet, preparing for the next step. Maybe Pat should come clean, tell it first—tell people his version: schoolyard fight, got a bit out of hand, didn't know anything about the wheelchair. Uncle Ted was dead and buried. The good old boy should take the rap. Would the party let him do that? The guy had been a model Whig. Pat's mind was calculating rapidly now. He needed more information; specifics instead of dark hints; he returned to his chair and sat.

"Okay, Miller. What'd Camel say exactly?"

"Nothing directly, but we've been piecing posts together like..." The man gestured vaguely.

"Like a crazy quilt?" Pat offered.

"What, sir?"

"Never mind. My wife...never mind. Go on."

"He calls himself The Worm and it's personal. However...uh. He's left some other hints. We think when he calls you he's going to make a personal demand. Of you."

"And?"

"And if you don't meet the demand, he's going to try and blow up industrial Houston."

Wow, Pat felt the blood drain out of his face. He was astonished. Unbelieving. "A bluff. Right?"

"Who knows. He's the top safety officer at Pythos Petrochemical. Whether or not he's good with demolitions, we don't know. 'Triggering Chain reaction' is the phrase. Jon Camel wasn't in the military, no criminal records. Clean. Like you."

Pat stared at him. "And you were military, Miller?"

"Army." Pat raised his eyebrows. "I was in the Far East Conflict, yes sir."

"Right. Well. Okay, well, this briefing of yours isn't much to go on."

"It's where we are right now, Governor."

Pat saw the man's thick hide now. Miller didn't look like ex-military. Pat preferred civilian machos, he could get on top of them with charm or sniff out their weak areas. But this man, like other warriors—as he thought of them—they were thick tough. You had to beat them on your own ground, not theirs.

"What else, Miller. No games, I need everything you've got."

"We don't play games, sir."

Pat got pissed and considered punishing Miller. Better not, he was in sticky enough piles of shit as it was. He sprang up and crossed over to the window. It faced southeast and he could see the edge of the vast array of lights demarcating Houston's petrochemical treasure sprawl. 'Chain reaction' kept running through his head. Chemistry wasn't his best subject. But the implication was clear: blow up one stick of dynamite, it'll blow any others nearby. The Petrochem. Boys always promised it couldn't happen—their safeties would prevent it, even if the plant next door caught fire. But, did he really want to bet on that, knowing these Boys as well as he knew them?

His gaze went up over a hazy line and he could pick out some stars. The three-line belt of Orion, he knew that one. A really bright star below it. Star gazing wasn't his best subject either. No Marta to ask.

"You were in the army, Miller, what's the really bright star?"

"Sirius, sir."

"Oh," he turned. He looked at the man's river otter face. Could he get this guy on his side? "You see action?" he tried.

"I did, sir."

He left it at that. Like a chum, he asked, "What can you tell me about Sirius?"

"You're serious?" Pat chuckled but the guy looked blank, so he just gave him a nod of encouragement. "It's in the constellation Canis Minor. It's the highest apparent magnitude star."

"Apparent?"

"Not the most luminous thing we see with the naked eye. But where it is, proximity to earth, the brightest."

The guy sounded like a science advisor. "That so. What's the second-brightest?"

"Canopus."

"You an astronomer, Miller?"

"No, sir, just part of the training."

And that was that. FBI sent Miller, Miller was probably the best, and Pat needed the best, but sometimes these people made him feel like, after all, his education and life experience hadn't been good enough. For a situation like this. Shit and fan. Was gusto enough to get things done?

A discreet warning knock sounded at the door.

"Okay, Miller. Time to go back in. Keep low about Camel for now. We'll see what surfaces. I'm going to use the facility."

"Yes, sir." Miller got up, went out and closed the door behind him.

Pat remained standing, his forehead and cheeks hot. He dabbed his cheeks with the backs of his cold hands, a weird sensation, his body both hot and cold. He didn't have to pee but it was standard procedure. If he never held office again and never had to sit through another meeting, that wouldn't be all bad. But the next thought killed it: he'd dry up without work. He laid a cold hand on his hot brow, knees weak and sinking. He pivoted and grabbed a chair back to keep from falling. But a moment later he crumpled to his knees—'My God,'—but before he could pray he was weeping....He called Marta's name softly, pinching the sobs...punching that poor kid down that long tube of memory, wanting to stop and not wanting to stop and not stopping and glad to deal vengeance...and now the victim was coming for him. The Worm...of all names, turning to destroy him. He was blind in a cold plunge boil.

Not sure how long he was there, when his mind came back to the present he trembled getting to his feet and wiped his face again, adjusted his belt.

In the bathroom, his pee burst out and sprayed the rim; somebody else would clean it up. He washed his face, slapped his cheeks, brushed his hair. Set his jaw. Stared at himself in the mirror: this is what a doer looks like, he reminded himself. He straightened his tie. Gusto.

He realized how hungry he was; the watermelon was long gone. No time. He headed for the wet bar and swallowed a belt of bourbon. Good. Phew. Okay. Let's take the call and take on this bastard. Beaten him once, beat him again. Bring it, Worm, bring it!

The argument about a 'clandestine' evacuation raged on, and **Mayeershaiana** felt the moisture along her lower back that often reminded her of that late summer by the Ganges in Varanasi when she was a boy, spent with her mother's family because her father was sick. Vivid colors and dancing. The hotel A/C wasn't up to the task of Houston's humidity and so many bodies in this room. What did they call it, a 'ballroom'? She couldn't imagine dancing here. A 'conference' room?

The Mayor and the Governor were shouting, name-calling, like children on the beach, edging closer to each other in the room until they seemed like they were in a crowd surrounded by abashed spectators.

Not sure if she had the authority to do so, she stood up and employed an advocacy technique, walking between the men and counting while turning in circles. The Governor went silent first, then the Mayor, and while the men stared at her like she was mad she said, "Constructive! I've got something constructive to add to this debate."

In the pause created she addressed the Mayor first. "I know there has been much information about what the Worm *might* be able to do and *might* be able to see, but understanding his motives will be important. He wants to feel in control. He wants to exercise power. If he feels betrayed after making a demand, or helpless in the face of an action, that is when he is likely to enter a psychotic frame of mind." The mayor seemed riveted by the word 'psychotic'.

"Meaning what?" the Governor barked from behind her. "Morals?"

She turned deliberately, expanding the lilt in her delivery. "Psychopaths can't relate to the feelings of others. If he is a psychopath, that would be the worst case, in my view. But whether or not his brain is emotionally damaged, I advise you to treat this as a game you are playing. A game, you see? It is a game and he is telling you the rules. You don't know the game very well, not so well as he does. When he tells you the rules, you have to take him literally. Literally," she repeated. "You cannot cheat, it's his game. You cannot interpret." She smiled faintly, pointing to show she understood his tendencies: "Aggression will bring trouble. Anger will bring trouble. I am afraid, sir, it's best to comply, or appear to comply, with exactly what he says. Oh, and mind you, you can't quit."

"We'll see about that," the Governor said. "What else?"

She noticed his eyes on her long black hair and knew she had gotten over the main obstruction. It was like getting out of a jam-packed street and now you could move at a reasonable pace and actually get somewhere. She nodded slightly at the Mayor to include him and she talked crisply.

"Let's consider the exact instructions so far, shall we?" She went back to her padlet. "I have the Worm's verified statements. I suggest we consider them rules." She projected onto the big screen and read the text out deliberately, like she did when lecturing first-years at the University:

"I'm the Worm. *(This is his name.)*" She interrupted briefly: "The italics are mine. Have you got it?

"I'm the Worm from your past. *(This is your relationship.)*"

"I'll call to deal at eleven. *(This is the schedule.)*"

"Time for a reckoning. *(This is what is at stake between you—the reason to play the game.)*"

"Is this the Hero of Houston? *(Hero of Houston is your name. Like a character name in a story. Or an avatar.)*"

"Careful what you say in public or I'll end the game. Have your briefing. But no mass evacuations. No deployments. No power outages. Anything like that, game over. Follow my instructions. Only then will Houston be safe. *(These are the rules that must be followed exactly.)*"

The Mayor and Governor had migrated together to see better. She made a gesture that included both men: "I believe these are the Worm's terms. His way of seeing things. They are rules of the game to follow. Literally."

The Mayor spoke first. "Not evacuating is a big risk." He sat down. He had regained his composure, nodding, "But I see, okay, okay, Mayeershaiana—" he pronounced her name correctly!—"So, you're saying he can't *see* anyone deploying—not police or SWAT. He can't *know* anyone is evacuating, but we could still move some key personnel or sensitive groups." He pointed at the police chief. "No public service messages, chief. But if traffic is a little heavier than usual..." The Mayor shrugged, heads nodded, a few other suggestions were made.

Meanwhile, the Governor was rooted to his spot, as if unwilling to let the fight go, as if the tickets had been bought and the show advertised and must go on, yet he wouldn't go along. Finally, the tall, well-looking head nodded. "That's your call, Mayor. You decide how to keep from provoking the nutcase. And I focus on the face to face." He edged nearer, as if to get a closer look...or maybe a sniff. Like an animal. "Isn't that right, ma'am?"

Mayeershaiana made a little noise of disapproval, tempted to yield ground. Instead, though, she bobbed in closer and shook her head a little in a way her grandmother used to when dealing with a difficult merchant in the market and pointed at the governor, hand held close to her body so it was inclusive rather than threatening. "You. You are the focus of the Worm, Governor. You have to play. The rest of us have to make sure we don't spoil the game before it starts." He stepped back. "It is disrespectful you know, calling him a nutcase—aggressive. This isn't a political game with an adversary you don't agree with. This is a crisis with a man who could be psychotic." She dropped her hand to her side. "Or at least, he's rejection sensitive. Surely emotionally damaged. Life in pain. Pain, you know, is hard on the brain."

He looked her up and down, like he was studying her sexuality and race the way some did. But better manners prevailed and he smiled a little, said 'thanks', and returned to his chair.

The mayor said, "You'll forward the routine so Technical can distribute it to everyone?" She nodded. "Okay, you heard the expert, take these as rules. Everybody load and get 'em to your people."

Steadson asked, "Okay, wait a second, let's say he's psycho, what do I do when I talk to him?"

"Or not do," she said. "First, we don't know about psychotic, but we believe he may be on the sociopathy spectrum."

"Like Hitler?"

"That's right. And like your next-door neighbor." She lectured a bit: "Sociopaths are not necessarily authoritarian world leaders. They are to be found anywhere. The Worm's psychiatric profile is not well-known, but my team agrees there are some markers in his messages. These markers point to a personality disorder." She felt the pressure of time and spoke more rapidly. "Narcissistic personality disorder is most likely." The room went silent. "I say this because some of the behavior suggests a personality in need of admiration. Narcissists have little or no empathy and over-react to criticism, rejection, or blame." She paused, letting this sink in, knowing that recent events in the United States supplied a potent example of this behavior. "Flattery, for example, would be a safe tactic."

"Flattery?" Steadson sounded incredulous. "I don't get it."

"Flattery," she said firmly. "For example—"

At that moment, a smart rang; she saw it was the governor's; from his face as he regarded it, she knew it was the Worm. She tensed up—it had all seemed abstract—an intervention and a lecture, but not a consult with a patient. Now, it was as if the patient was banging on her office door.

The Governor held the screen toward her, confirming the caller. "Do I answer as 'Hero'?" he asked sarcastically.

She spoke flat, stiff-lipped like a Brit., "Sarcasm is aggressive, Governor." She could see him wrestle with his anger. "Humor is only safe if it's on his terms, not yours."

Steadson shrugged a little and settled on, "Hello." There was a pause, and then he threatened, "You don't fool me, Camel."

Pat felt the anticlimax as he looked at the blank smart. Shock could be seen on the faces in the room as he clicked off. "He hung up," he said, annoyed at the critical faces and at his sarcastic bravado. "No instructions, no demands, nothing."

Rival voices pitched in, but the Psych. lady held up her hand and Steadson made a sour face, but he gave her the floor and Tuck told everyone to shut up and they did.

"Rules!" the lady said, pointing at him. He pushed down the frustration and waited for the blow. "The game won't run unless you follow the rules."

"Like what?" he complained.

"First, don't use any name except the name he's adopted."

"This is juvenile, I have to call him Mr. Worm?" Some chuckles. The Psych. lady wasn't chuckling; she was a disquieting figure, so slight and unflappable—delicate even...maybe gay?

"I think you could call him 'Worm.'"

He realized bluff wasn't going to work; it might be a game, but it was serious. Had he blown it? No, there would be another chance, and he'd better bone up. "Okay, okay."

"Did he say anything at all?"

Pat was embarrassed, all those people watching, and he'd botched the call. Darn, he had to get hold of himself. In a low voice he said, "Okay, where's the techie? Rig this to a speaker so next time everybody gets it." He tossed the guy the smart—how old was he, twenty? Geez. "Okay, no, there was no conversation, it went like this. I said 'Hello', he asked, 'Is this the Hero of Houston?' and you heard what I said. And he hung up." He paused, held up his hands.

"Right, he is establishing the psychology of the hierarchy. You're at the apex, the 'Hero'. He's at the nadir, the 'Worm'. There are various tropes associated with the worm."

His prejudice, he knew, was that psychology was a fancy word for people manipulating people. He'd spent his whole career at the game, but maybe this woman knew something he needed. He asked, "You mean like the worm will turn? What about that?"

"I was thinking more, 'Don't Tread on Me'. Regardless, the implication of both is a reversal of fortune."

"I get it. You mean revenge. He wants revenge on me."

"Or justice might be a better word." The Governor felt his head sharply turn as he stared at her, probed her dark eyes gazing back without wavering.

He replied, "What do you mean?"

"Justice takes the moral high ground, Governor. That might be how you go from hero to...criminal. The Worm has taken some power, some leverage, by posing a threat. Be careful about discarding his power, he could end the game, as he calls it."

Pat saw the sense of that. "I got you now."

Someone in the room asked, "Do you think he'll call back or what?"

The Psych lady didn't answer. The police chief added, "He'll keep calls short so they can't be traced."

"Twenty seconds, you think nobody was listening, Hank?" The police chief shut his mouth tight. "He's gonna call back," Pat said, thinking aloud. "It's personal. He hasn't got what he wants out of me yet. If he wanted to blow up a bomb, he'd've blown it up. Correct?" Pat looked around, no one answered; a little aggression usually got people in line. He gestured at the Psych. lady—couldn't remember her name, something weird, where did Julio find these people? Cancel that, this lady was smart and could help.

The woman replied, "There is always a risk they will retaliate."

The police chief blurted out, "Sir, if this is so personal, do you know who this guy is?"

Pat avoided Miller in the corner while answering the chief. "It was a tactic," he said, a half-truth, the kind of thing he did all the time. But the chief was spun up now and wouldn't leave it alone.

"We need every bit of info we can get, Governor. Now if you—"

The smart rang before he could finish. It was a strange number. "Where does he get these numbers, the Chinese?"

"The Russians," the CIA guy said.

"Quiet, please." Pat clicked and talked into the smart: "Hello, Worm, this is the Hero of Houston."

Like the other times he'd called, the Worm spoke in a reedy, childish voice, embedded in strange background static. But with the speakers, everyone in the room would be able to hear.

"Well then, Hero" resounded the voice, "Here we go." After a brief pause, words came quicker than before, as if some of the 'fun' had gone out of it: "Come to Gate B at Pythos. Alone. Midnight. If you're late or don't show, the game is up."

Reading the faces in the room, **Mayeershaiana** knew that she was now spurious. Maybe that was for the best—it was a limited psychiatric profile, and she suspected the Worm's communications were deliberately deceptive. Time was the bastard now; cool analysis had backed down. Her idea of 'rules' had been accepted, her advice given. She knew a diagnosis wasn't as helpful as an open mind; Pat Steadson didn't seem a particularly good candidate for that.

She watched him and the Mayor puffing up, delegating, defining, cajoling and soothing and thanking. Others hid their anxiety in furtive nods and quick exits. She allowed herself to pull back and reflect. 'Unperturbed' her teachers called it. She noted the governor's eyes resting on her, as if he wanted to ask her something, and she waited, but he made no sign. She wondered why the mayor's office had requested her in the first place and not the Dean. She was quite junior and no experience with political types, but maybe somebody realized that Governor Steadson butted heads with men and tended to ease down and listen to women. This analysis, she thought wryly, was not ironic and crude.

Her nose itched. The ring there reminded her of home. She was conscious she was the only person in the room wearing vibrant colors—red and orange. Most everyone else was navy blue, grey, black. The FBI bloke dark brown. She smiled to herself—what if she had painted a red tip on her forehead? Mother would have done something like that! It would have given these men...she verified there was only one other woman left in the room...pause. Most wouldn't know what the third eye signified. Most would feel atavistic suspicion and some might grow officious. She had never worn a tip as decoration anyway, it was mostly the idea of how different Houston people were from Bengaluru: particularly Mother and her Committee for Streets. Mother was such a useful reference in these situations. She would have been proud that Mayeershaiana didn't shorten her name for her students or these officials, even if it wasn't her given name.

Would the Governor develop his own strategy against the aggressor? The University had been a haven and a border; she had never visited this part of downtown. Could these blokes handle a crisis? The Worm—was he capable of...if this bomb exploded, and the damage occurred...? She shuddered. It could be the greatest ecological disaster in history. It might destroy the entire Gulf ecosystem. Then what would the governor do?

'Also,' she thought, 'What would I do? I know nothing about ecology and geography. I know that Texas is large—280,000 square miles. But small compared to India's million square miles. Houston...a third of Bengaluru's eight million people.' She stopped these comparisons. She missed her family suddenly. Depending on what happened tonight, it might be time to return home and, at last, face her past. Steadson was surely about to face his.

The governor wasn't coming over. She tidied her belongings but didn't get up in case someone else had more questions. She looked around, placid. The police chief was leaving the room talking loudly on his smart, followed by the fire chief, a sad-looking man who looked ill. Then there were the serpents in the corner, licking their lips, jab-talking at a lawyer whose face never changed expression. The Mayor and his people left next, having forgotten they'd called her in, she imagined. The governor was dismissing the man from the CIA, who looked unhappy.

"No National Guard I said, you hear?" Steadson's voice rang out the command, the kind her uncle used against her when, as a young man, she defied her family's plans for university. It had simply made her stronger, though, having someone to defy. Would the CIA listen to a governor, or defy him? "Go do something useful somewhere else," Steadson growled. The CIA man snatched his coat and stomped out.

A man in fatigues approached him, holding out a gun; the governor raised a hand and turned toward her and said, "Ma'am, you can go. Keep your smart on in case we need you."

Mayeershaiana nodded. "Right. I will be available at any hour, sir."

"Good, don't sleep tonight," he said, somewhat warmly, she thought as she got to her feet. To her surprise, he had come all the way across the room, leaving the man and his gun behind along with the serpents, who also wanted his attention, but for now he ignored them. "Any last-minute advice?" he whispered, leaning close. "I'm going into the lion's den." He paused, a flicker of vulnerability in his eyes. "Know what I mean?"

She responded to his charm and his alarm. "Yes. I mean, I have heard of the lion's den before, though I don't know its origin."

"Book of Daniel. The Bible." He paused.

"Oh I see. Well I am a Hindu, and I have not read the Bible. But I can guess what you mean." He was looking at her steadily, so close she could smell him, a ripened fruit smell. His large hands were on his hips—he took his space, as men often do. She was not influenced, however, and as before didn't yield and remained unperturbed as she chose her words carefully. "Governor, do you know this man?"

He hesitated. "Yes," he said. "But keep it between us."

She thought quickly, "And you...caused this man harm somehow."

"Yes, I...I didn't realize how much."

"And he blames you personally for something?" She was guessing, but the governor's face was surprisingly open—he was capable of that after all, increasing his chances of success. "Something that shaped his life." It wasn't even a question.

"Dead on."

"Then revenge is not out of the question. Simple revenge. You have to pay. I mean, that may be his thought process."

"I've dealt with little men like him before. Inferiority thing. But I..." He paused. "I don't have ammo, if you see what I mean. He's holding almost all the cards—I need a few."

"Right. He is trying to establish a superior position. Superior justice. But you can fight that."

"How? You mean with flattery like you said? What else?"

"With goodness."

The governor blinked. He hadn't expected that! He almost said something, then he raised a hand, as if he wanted to place it on her shoulder or to touch her long sleek hair; instead, he shook her hand, his grip firm, the hand large and warm. Finally, he said, "Thanks, ma'am, I'll keep that in my pocket." And then his long legs were striding away from her and back to the military man and his gun.

Mayeershaiana felt herself cast down despite being of service. She adjusted her purse and padlet and got up to leave; no one was looking at her any more. The snakes had eyes only for the governor as she crossed the room. A security man was holding the door, readying to close it behind her but not looking at her directly. If she were still a man, she thought, or white, he probably would. She exercised a clinical glance over her shoulder as the door was closing: Governor Steadson was nodding at the advisor with the gun and flashing a grin of confidence; interactions in Mayeershaiana's brain told her not to believe.

The bulky ballistics guy was still talking but **Pat** was thinking about what the Psych. lady had said about goodness. It had been like stinging tonic after a shave. He was not paying much attention to the .40 caliber handgun, his brain asserting pistols were all much the same. However, the guy finally shut up and clearly wanted him to take the weapon, so he did. It was small for its power, and light—he immediately disliked the non-metallic sensation. The first time he ever shot was a .22 pistol in Jasper back in the woods; boy, that gun had been a heavy hunk of metal. Back then, he was ten years old with flimsy arms and weak wrists. He'd bulked up after that, and he'd grown like crazy. He stared at the plastic thing in his grip and knew he didn't really want it. He might ditch it. If Camel let him bring it inside, it was probably useless anyway. Military had insisted, but he deemed it a waste of time.

He waved at the Security Chief, ordered, "Stu, get my AP." To the ballistics guy, he said, "I need to do this first, hang on." Lynn was there like magic, ready for instruction, professional. He reckoned he'd spent more minutes of waking life with her than with Marta. How old was she now, 35? Never talked about her personal life, but he dreaded the day she got married or, Lord help him, pregnant. "Lynn, I need to get everything put together in my smart. All the briefs."

She nodded. "I already told I.T. Shouldn't be ten minutes and I'll get it loaded."

"Great. Sorry it's a late night."

"I don't get paid for the hours I work, I get paid to get the work done," she said, her usual response when he apologized. He didn't really know what they paid her. Not enough. He should look into it.

"That your secretary, Guv?" ballistics guy was asking as she walked off.

"Associate Partner," Pat said it mildly, a gentle nudge to come into the current society, but the old-school ballistics guy was staring at her ass and didn't seem to hear. "How many extra cartridges you giving me?" Pat asked. The guy replied in ballistics jargon, but part of Pat's brain was already jumping ahead to the next confrontation with the FBI guy.

Miller watched the Governor running a hand through his hair; thick, it all stood up and remained, like he'd put gel in it. He seemed to realize this and patted it down and then heaved himself out of the comfy chair, not once giving Miller a glance. They had been in the suite almost five minutes—valuable seconds Miller could use were vanishing! Getting Steadson to the rendezvous on time was tighter and tighter. But the governor's doss. showed he insisted on private time, 'To gather his composure'. In Miller's book, the Guv liked to make you wait. Thousands of people awaiting orders. Him, too.

But still, Miller suppressed his disgust, ignoring the vibes from his smart; he liked keeping it strapped at his hip and not up to his face; some agents didn't even see what room they were in they spent so much of their bandwidth getting interrupted. He could usually ignore the smart when it was on his belt, but now the thing was spinning like a neutron star: regular pulses, non-stop. The whole situation was like that, spinning fast. Easy for the brain to get dizzy. A guy like Camel would know he didn't have much time before Miller's types got to him one way or the other; the cripple had his 'foot' on the accelerator.

But...better to get orders late so long as they were precise, concise, smart. Better to wait until the Guv knew his own mind. Miller had experience with civilians changing their minds three times at the outset of a big operation, not grasping the dangerous interconnections every order entailed. Worse a piecemeal-boss than a wait-boss.

Steadson had walked to the window after getting up; he seemed to be looking up at the night sky. Were they going to have another astronomy chat? With his back to him, the Guv finally offered up, "We never met until tonight, but I reckon you're a patient man, Miller."

"Sometimes, Governor." Some edge to that comment, Miller thought he'd better keep a check on his impatience. "Sometimes."

"I just don't know what else to do, frankly." Miller almost gaped at this admission, this bit of honesty from a politician! "Let's start with something easy. The gun: should I take it?" He had taken the pistol from its sheath and was waggling it in the air to one side; the man had large hands and the weapon looked like a toy.

"Can you handle a weapon?"

"Eh. It's been a while, but sure. Safety...cartridge..." Even from behind, the Guv looked at home with it—maybe he was downplaying his knowledge.

"Then I'd take it," Miller said calmly. After all, it was a toss-up—best to sound decisive. He didn't figure it was going to help or harm. The Worm was in a wheelchair; the conflict wasn't going to be decided by a firefight, despite the squeals from the national guard colonel earlier. The Governor had sniffed out that puppy right away. Miller nearly grinned, recalling the Governor's saying loud enough for the guy to hear, 'Get this warmonger out of my hotel room before he hurts somebody.' Then he'd driven off the CIA guy. That had been fun.

He was curious what else the Guv would ask...besides the obvious. But again, the boss was not rushing; he was over there thinking, putting the gun slowly in its sheath and buckling it in, and looking up again at the stars before they vanished in the gathering clouds. The smart was vibrating again. Without sounding too urgent, he asked, "What else can I do to help, sir?"

"You're not going to release Camel's identity?"

There, the elephant in the room. If the Bureau knew, other people knew, and it would be hard for the Guv to keep it under wraps. Still, that wasn't the immediate problem. "I'm not going to release it, no. Neither is the Bureau, not at this time. We're just lining up everything so we can take him down."

The Guv said, "I know what you're thinking, Miller." Miller looked around, as if he might see something he'd missed before. "It won't be long until it gets out. One way or another." He paused but Miller didn't want to answer him.

The guy was thinking about his career, he supposed, and that was a factor. What if this big tough-talking politician was really a coward and walked away and the bomber really could and did blow up half of Houston? Miller had seen the numbers. Houston could be rebuilt, assuming that could be done before sea-level rise made it moot. But the Gulf would remain a toxic lagoon for a decade unless somebody came up with some real clever bio-disaster cleanup miracle. He'd heard fungi could do wonders, but he wasn't convinced.

Everything was short-term to these politicians. A year ahead to another election was the most they planned for, as best he could tell, but mostly it was all about this week. Miller hated that crap. His hard-ass career military dad had taught him to focus on the best choice overall, not the number of obstacles to it. He tried not to worry about consequences; he would rather be able to sleep at night...well, when the death swamp action wasn't keeping Julia up wiping sweat off his forehead and holding him until the shakes stopped. Miller set his jaw—he was fine, getting better. He was going to kick it without doctors or treatments.

Anyway, it was going to be a long night for him and the Guv and a lot of other people. He'd already notified Julia and sent her to stay with her mother in San Antonio: "Don't worry, *mi corazón*. Ticket's under your name. Get a cab, go, don't ask. *Besos*." Miller kept in shape for these kinds of nights. Excitement was good, it buoyed him against the drag of depression. Enough to feed his adrenaline habit but not too much to send him over into the crazy place. And with Julia safe on a plane, he could focus on babysitting this civilian, staying alive, and finishing the mission.

Don knew that the Party bosses didn't want to talk to him. It was late, they had consulted with legal and given their 'suggestions' to the Guv and their minions, which they believed were orders, and for their trouble they'd been told to get out of everybody's way.

J.J. complained, "Genius in charge. We'll sleep good and see what blew up in the mornin', heh." The old vulture, with his red beak and puckered lips. When neither Boston nor Chambers laughed, he got grumpy and was first getting out the door.

That was perfect, Don thought, he'd rather talk to the younger two. How old was Boston, maybe 40? And Chambers, early 50s, definitely, with kids in college he vaguely recalled—probably all as ugly as their father. Both men were shaking his hand and thanking him for helping the Guv and being a good Lieutenant and all that kind of stuff. Little did they know Don's secret and his scheme, practically burning a hole through the top of his head; they couldn't dream this was the chance of his lifetime! He sucked in a fateful breath and took stock just as both men turned for the door: is this the moment? Fuck it, he just let himself go and he was talking and going out the door with them—

"Gentlemen, listen, we got another problem. And it's big. I need your advice before you go."

"Sure, Tuck," Chambers said.

Boston nodded, a bit surprised, and held up a hand and said, "You want me to call back J.J.—?"

But Don didn't need to nix the idea, Chambers was already doing it. "Let's not bother old J.J., why don't we get a drink in the bar."

Don hesitated. "I would most times, but...it's gotta be private."

Chambers hardly missed a beat. "My car then."

Boston chuckled a little. "Tuck, if I get in trouble over stayin' out late, you're apologizin' to the wife in person, ya hear?"

"Sure."

They were silent in the elevator down. The lobby was deserted except for dazed-looking desk staff and the unobtrusive security guards. Chambers 'good-nighted' pleasantly and led Don and Boston out to the valet box. Boston made small talk while they waited for the car; he covered weather and sports and was undeterred by zero verbal response. Boston put his arm over Don's shoulders and asked, "Hell, Tuck, when's the last time you and Laura came out? We gotta do that. They got you chained to your desk in Austin? What about a three-day weekend thing? Isn't there one comin' up this month?"

Don was nodding and smiling: "I'd like that, Bossy."

Chambers was looking straight ahead and Don realized the man knew about Laura filing for divorce; Boston was at a lower level. That's what it was about, climbing up the levels. And he was about to propose a leap. Would Chambers and his cronies go for it? Would they hold it against him for not being patient? J.J. was hard to read. But Chambers liked the young bucks. The nomination was wide open. The Guv was the obvious choice. But after tonight, the Guv might be a dead dog politically; or, he might just be dead.

The car came around. Don realized how shitty he'd felt for months now that he was about to launch his audacious plan. The crumbling marriage was awful. He could find another woman, he figured, and would get over Laura, but he couldn't replace seeing his kids.

The valet held the door for Chambers; get in back, and let the boys hear him whisper the secrets and propose the deal from behind? No, he bolted around and beat Boston to the front passenger door. "Come on, Bossy, I'm talkin'," he said lightly. Boston punched him on the arm and got in the back. A jock, that's what Bossy was, really. Not Chambers—Chambers was a grinder.

"I'll pull around the back and park," Chambers said and edged into the street and whipped around the hotel lot and squeezed into a bare spot between hulking pickup trucks. He turned off the engine A waiting silence.

Don rubbed his hands together nervously. "Uh, gentlemen, uh..."

"We're listening," Chambers said, a bit patronizingly.

Don flared up and barked, "Pat Steadson got in a fight, okay, with that terrorist bomber when they were kids. Beat him up so bad it paralyzed the bastard." Boston woo-wheed in the backseat; Chambers stayed quiet. "Couldn't control his temper. Poor guy wanted his fair turn on the baseball diamond, came at him with a stick. Steadson wouldn't share. Punched him 30 times, put him in a wheelchair for life. That story's under wraps but it could get out. Probably will get out. I don't think it'd do his...political aspirations a whole lotta good."

"Goddammit!" Chambers hit the steering wheel. "This goddam party is a goddam leaky boat! Who knows besides us?"

"I got a private source. Secure. If the Guv gets lucky, maybe he beats this bastard again, maybe the story can get buried or shot down. But if the Guv isn't lucky...the party might be in deep shit if they endorsed him. Remember what happened two years ago?"

"Goddammit, Tuck, quit talkin' like we're stupid."

Don was surprised to see the temper Chambers kept hidden most of the time. "I like to be blunt," he defended himself. "I like my message to be clear."

"Oh it's clear, goddammit!"

"Clear as a stampede," Bossy supplied from the back seat.

"No." Don paused. "No, there's more." The two men stared and Don felt like throwing back his head and laughing. By the balls! He had them! He had the Guv! "If Steadson gives up the nomination, I want it."

Boston started to guffaw and stopped and then whistled. Chambers' reaction was hard to read. He said quietly, "What you want, Tuck, and what the Party wants are two different things."

"I'm the Guv's right hand man. I was second-team All American at U.T. I won Mr. Telegenic at the Convention." He paused. "Maybe it's not two different things."

"Goddam, Tuck, you got some bull-sized balls," Boston said, admiringly.

"Get a cab home, will ya Bossy?" Chambers asked.

"Ahhh..sure, Nick. Sure, course. Well, well, uh, good night, Gents." Boston fussed a bit but squeezed out of the car and sauntered back toward the valet.

Chambers pressed the ignition. "Four Seasons?" he asked.

"Alessandra."

Traffic was light. The Alessandra was only a few blocks away and Chambers talked quickly. "Tuck, you got nice suits. You got potential. But I'm telling you, you're jumping the gun."

"Listen—"

"No, you listen. Is the divorce done?"

"No."

"Can you get it un-done with your wife?"

"I don't see how that'd help, the court's already got it."

"Don't worry about the court, we'll worry about the court. Can you get it un-done with her?"

Don hadn't expected this. "I don't know."

"You willing to try?" Don's thoughts fired—beg Laura? Beg the lawyer? Get back in that cold bed? "I asked you a question, Donald, give me an answer—you didn't think about this?"

"Not...exactly." Don kept laser-focus: of course he would try, for his kids, yes, for his career, yes. So what if Laura's legal had figured the Atlanta hush money...why would she want anyone to know? Unless she'd been telling her girlfriends...he certainly wasn't going to let Chambers in on it. Or the Party.

"What's the reason on file for your divorce?" Chambers asked. "Don't tell me it's personal. What's the reason?" Don hesitated, not sure how to answer, knowing it was key. "Goddammit, Tuck, come clean with me. Did you get caught cheating on her?"

Don chose his words carefully. "Unreconcilable differences."

"Uh huh." Chambers pulled over to the curb a block short of the Alessandra Hotel and stabbed the brake; they jolted to a stop. Chambers jabbed a pointer finger, not too close, but close enough. "You find out how irreconcilable, and you report back to me, and then we'll talk again. Good night." Don thanked him and got out of the car. Chambers lurched away—he was in for a long night now, too.

Looking up, Don noticed the thunderheads—he could feel the air thickening. Smiling and humming, he walked toward the brightly-lit Alessandra lobby as the first flashes of lightning stroked the sky above its flat rooftop.

He was all jacked up, like after a pot of coffee, and his hands jumped busily in his pockets until they grasped the door handles, only for the automated rotary motor to swing them in a circle for him, the carpet red and laid before him all the way to the concierge desk, three smiling guys fighting to hand him his key card. He tipped the one who managed to win out. Humming again, he went for the elevator and, again, the door opened for him, and he stepped inside and briefly glanced at the card because he'd forgotten which floor it was. But the elevator had already chosen for him, reading the key, supposedly, and he hummed louder: how easy everything was going to be from now on!

Soon, the doors shooshed open and he looked at the card again because the doors all looked alike, but out of the corner of his eye, he saw a light blinking on a doorway to his left. Smiling, shaking his head at technology, he strolled to it and waved the plastic thing and the door clicked and popped open an inch. He went inside.

Em had slipped out of his mind but of course she was there. In short shorts and a lacy black top, legs crossed, reading by the window. Her legs looked like candy. Chambers' accusatory question, 'Did you get caught cheating on her?' played back. Don looked around guiltily: were these rooms surveilled? He shut the drapes—another hotel stood across the street and God knows it wouldn't take much for some brazen reporter to zoom in and—

"Hey baby," Em said in a lazy drawl.

"Hey," he answered, trying to sound at ease, unable to resist looking at the smooth, shiny flesh of her thighs. His tongue rubbed against his front teeth.

She uncrossed her legs; dark eyes scanned his and then slowly traveled back to the book propped up on her bare knees. She was tilted forward and delightful masses of flesh shifted behind the lace. Images from the last two nights repeated pleasantly; he swallowed, his desire hardening. He had begged her on his knees to come to Houston with him...after her first 'no' he had ached...sex with Em was erotic and, he realized, addictive. Now what? His big career chance had blossomed out of nowhere and, like syrup on top of syrup, here she was, a few sweet feet away from him.

"Long day?" she asked, turning a page, not seeming to care if he responded.

"Every day in politics is long," he snapped out the cliché. She didn't look up but kept reading. He liked that about her—she was gracious but didn't pry and probably didn't really care. The machinations and maneuvers, his ambitions, the fateful decisions made every day...did not touch her. Her detachment from affairs of state was enviable: she didn't suffer the stress or the losses. And, she was a good capitalist: she expected payment in advance of service.

"I think I'll take a shower," he said, hoping by the time he finished he'd know what to do and what not to do.

Chapter 3: The Game at Pythos

Pat stood at the delivery gate for Pythos Petrochemical's Refinery and checked his smart: it was six minutes before midnight, a mere nine miles from the safety of the hotel downtown, and yet another world...Southeast Houston. Pat counted only two times he'd been in this part of town. Pythos' round ranks of massive tanks and stacks exhaled smoke and steam, hulking among the scummy green bayous, a vast overground and underground complex of toxic high-pressure chemical gases and liquids. With a lightning storm charging inland. And a terrorist with a match. Dang.

He'd visited Lyonn down the block once and recognized Chuw's logo across the way. Along with Pythos, a devilish triangle they made in the artificial light, a bizarre human-made jungle holding most of the energy of his political career and for all of Texas. According to the briefing, Pythos had a single after-hours security person on duty. One person! Everything else by computer. The computer had been notified about the Worm but not the security guy. Dang again.

The stuffy wet humidity confirmed the weather report: the first few fat raindrops of the predicted storm fell, tentatively at first, then steady and hard on his bare head. He hummed awhile and a tune came into his mind and he remembered a night Laird was away with Marta's parents—date night, they used to call it—and they were dancing in the living room, bobbing to Link Wray's guitar...happy...free...and then making love, first on the stairs...Marta started it, taking off her blue blouse with a playful teasing toss of the head...the tender bliss of kissing her lips...

Pat looked down at his hands. He shouldn't think about Marta now, he should just follow his instincts. No sex since she got sick. What, six years? 'Darn Okie, don't die on me.' Why had he said that—couldn't he have thought up something sweeter? Sorrow threatened sometimes to bend him in half. It could sweep in like a gale out of nowhere among prairie grass. He forced himself to stand tall, but his hands were against his face, and tears near. He missed touching. And for some reason, that woman, with the weird name...something Asian...Bangladesh?—the Psych. lady in red with the proud nose and dark eyes and the smooth forehead, long silky hair...she and Senator Mack had sure stirred up something. And here he was, in deep trouble, death lurking, fantasizing what it would be like to slowly rake his fingers through those women's dark hair. Uncle Ted would have propped either of them, but Pat had always believed in marriage. Still, what would it be like? Nowadays, a man had to be extra careful. God, what was wrong with him?

He looked up and found the star, not yet obscured by the storm boiling out of the Gulf...Sirius. How far away was it? How long had it been there? It gleamed, cold. But stars, he knew, were hot. How hot? Miller wasn't there to tell him. Hotter than he could imagine. A light passed—a meteor? A satellite? A helicopter...silent. Darn, they'd better be careful! Then came the first grumble of thunder, like a warning. Forking cracks lit up the southeastern horizon. The rain slacked, a brief respite—the storm was coming.

He got angry-impatient suddenly, tempted to call in an airstrike. No—bad idea, talk about knocking down all the dominoes. The plan was in motion. He had to step up and play his part. Do his duty. Wait and get wet.

He recalled the bosses after the briefing, patting his shoulders, telling him he'd make it fine. Easy for them—they'd go sit in some hotel room or in their living rooms and watch sports highlights. Or they'd fall asleep and see what the news report said in the morning about Pat Steadson and Jon Camel...Worm, the nutcase bastard. What time was it? Two minutes to midnight. As if Midnight was some sacred or unholy number. A silly game. At one time in his life, he'd thought everything was a game and every game was about securing and sustaining the next level. What did he think now about whether he was advancing in the game?

The smart rang—damnation! Gus Pierhl, Lyonn CEO, millionaire, supporter! And jerk. Pat blocked the number. That was that. Maybe politics lay behind him. Maybe beating up a bully all those years ago would benefit him. Or maybe, if he could win through tonight, maybe, maybe, maybe (there was always the unpredictable element of notoriety) this adventure would shoot him to the top.

Almost time. Midnight in...10 seconds. He waited...it struck. Nothing. Except rain easing, the storm teasing with a few more thunder rumblers. He looked around. Security cameras, lights, the sighing-hum of the plant. The gate itself was a high-tech affair, with a sort of robot arm and eye. Thirty seconds past Midnight, the raindrops suddenly pelted down—like that machine-made movie rain that never looks like real rain, like someone turned everything up to high. He was soaked. Should he move over to that shelter beside the gate? Nothing was happening. He'd explicitly ordered the police chief not to give him any info about deployments, but he assumed there were men stationed out there somewhere, though he hadn't seen any signs. In the distance, he saw lightning dancing above a very tall tank over on the Lyonn property. Was hydrogen in that tall tank, he wondered? He thought back to the junk message he'd gotten about hydrogen and realized he hadn't shown it to the Psych lady. Too late.

Fifty seconds past...rain lashing him...what a night to be outside...he kept his eye on the lightning. The rain rose and fell in waves, some waves louder and faster, then the briefest sigh out before another round of crazy beats, and it looked like there were a thousand-thousand tiny puddles on the blacktop while drops rebounded in a wild dance as if they had hit tiny springs. He wiped his eyes. He thought of Leo, waiting for Leo to call, Leo's low voice. A sort of pneumatic huff and ching got his attention...the gate opened ponderously before 12:02 could strike. It widened steadily and stopped at the width of a car.

He sloshed forward and the gate closed behind him. Ahead was a long two-lane road; his AP had said they measured it as being close on half a mile. It ended in the main plant entrance. He looked at the smart—nothing. He shrugged and, with deliberate steps, strode forward. He gazed straight ahead, even though he felt eyes on him from the sides. Was Jon Camel watching him? Probably. He wanted to get this over with and quickened his pace.

A sound like a strangulated dog bark came from between buildings on his right; out of a side road came an electric car, stopping about a yard short of running him down. He peered in—a driverless. Darn, he didn't like this world sometimes. Distrusted machines, always had, seemed crazy to trust software when personal computers always had bugs and crashes.

The passenger door made a quiet 'pop' and opened a few inches. He nudged it, climbed inside, and wiped the rain off his face. A bunch of oog-ly digital lights were flashing, the door locked, an automatic seatbelt fastened, and then the car surged forward and topped out at exactly 20 miles per hour.

"Beats walking, I guess," he said aloud. The car, however, did not answer. Nor did it have wiper blades; the rain was falling hard now. A 'vvv' sound veeved in front of him and the car activated a screen built in to the dashboard which ran an educational video on driverless electric cars, the future of America and the World. It was like the seatbelt and emergency exit safety crap on an airline flight. Pat snorted, but looking out the window revealed blurry lights. The dashboard flashed something that looked like computer code—the gauges may have said 'fruit loops' for all the good they did him. "Won't bother me," he vowed out loud.

He sat helpless as the car trundled along. I.T. had given him an extra battery for his smart and he was perplexed as to why. "Well, feller could like well ya know, kill your signal, so..." 'Feller', he had thought, was an odd word for a tech expert to use. So in other words, Pat was prepared to be helpless. He figured it was his brain and his gut that he needed. Not the gun, not the smart, not insight on the safety of driverless cars. Camel was luring him back to the schoolyard...for a reckoning. Pat said a quick silent prayer and did what he hated doing: waited.

The car closed in on the front of the plant but veered off before it got there, down a narrow drive, and after a few tight turns a black wall rose up and the rain stopped and they were down a ramp and underground in darkness. He had noticed the headlights go out at the same time as the ramp opened up. Of course, maybe the computer didn't need light, but he became disoriented. He pulled out the smart, and the battery was draining fast—down to 30%. Sure enough, no signal. Battery to 12%. Wow, okay, the car turned in the black tunnel, and the smart battery plunged to 0%. Useless.

He wouldn't have been that surprised if Camel had introduced something into the car that rendered the handgun inert, too. Maybe that was a little too science-fiction-y. The good thing about the gun was maybe if Camel planned torture, he could take a quick way out. Like the Nazis and their cyanide capsules, he thought grimly.

The car was still going 20 miles per hour in darkness except what glow the displays cast on the shiny concrete walls. Like driving through a modern version of hell, he thought. Here he was, the most important man in Texas, playing a silly game in a dungeon. Still, he was surprised at how calm he was.

The car glided to a stop. The doors unlocked with a pop and the dome light came on. Nothing else. Cautiously, Pat opened the door and stepped out. Tiny dots of light, like a runway track, ended in a metal door. He looked down the tunnel he'd come through—he could just walk back out of here, right? Back up into the rain and the storm, find a cab, or just walk back to civilization. It was tempting. He could use his smart as a light...no, the battery was dead. Should he swap batteries? Or would that one drain too? Why hadn't they issued him a flashlight? Why rely on this stupid piece of plastic, dragging along with him wherever he went, giving no peace? He looked at the display: 0% battery, must shut down. And it chimed and shut down. That was that. Was anyone following him? Probably not. Probably they had been keeping track of him with the GPS and hoping for the best. He shut the car door. The driverless whirred, shot forward, and disappeared into darkness.

It smelled like a tent that hadn't been aired down here, he thought. He took a breath and followed the lights to the metal door. A grey pad hung crookedly beside it. He waited. After a minute, he barked out, "Hello? I'm waiting." Seconds, then a minute passed. He shifted his weight and looked around. It was so grim-dark except for the little runway lights, he didn't dare wander beyond. The door edges admitted no light. He talked to the door, asking it to open, etcetera, but that didn't do anything. He reconsidered swapping the smart battery. The gun was still there, at his side, but useless in the circumstances. Was this a test of some kind? He was getting irritated.

Then a 'tunk' sound brought his attention back to the door, which slid open. He stepped cautiously into a small box beyond, which triggered a door to slide shut. He was inside an elevator. It plunged down. The hell image returned to his mind. About ten seconds passed and, suddenly, before the elevator had completely stopped, the door slid open again about three-quarters of the way. Peering out, it was apparent the elevator had stopped part-way between floors. There was a space to crawl through up to a lighted, plush carpeted area; or a black void below. He waited. The elevator didn't move.

He started to swear and stopped himself. Finally, with a shrug, he reached out and crawled up onto the carpet. He stood erect, dusting off his slacks, and looked around. It was a large space, like a banquet room, with recessed lighting and a panoramic plexiglass window on one side, though nothing could be seen beyond. How tedious—where was the little bastard? Closed doors stood at either end. He trudged one way—locked. He trudged back the other way—locked; he rapped—nothing. The elevator door shut with a snick.

"Wild goose chase," he muttered out loud. He couldn't see another exit. Feeling defiant, he leaned against the wall, folded his arms, scowled (so that if the Worm had a camera he'd see his dissatisfaction), and waited

He waited but it was quiet and there was almost no sound detectable down here beneath the lifeless Petro Patch. He thought about the quiet evenings watching Leo sleep until Laird and Jesse swung by to pick her up. Pretty Miss with her bunny. "You *want* to babysit?" he almost chuckled remembering Jesse's words of disbelief. Of course he wanted to spend every free minute with her! But he wouldn't say that. He wouldn't admit that Qwifall, without Marta, was a lonely place. Oh, that name. 'That some Okie word?' he'd teased. 'Maybe,' she'd said. But Marta called their home Qwifall and it would always be Qwifall, however big and empty.

His eyes grew heavy. He heard a click and the door at the far end had inched open. Wearily, suppressing a curse, he paced to the far end, half-expecting the door to close before he got there, but it didn't. He pulled it open. He was faced with a narrow concrete alcove sporting three utility doors and a metal desk built into the wall, like a security station. He felt like he'd checked into the bowels of a gas chamber—it was creepy. Was that the faint smell of something chemical? Was he to be poisoned? He tried the left door, locked. Middle door, locked. Right door, unlocked; he yanked it open.

Beyond lay a medium-sized room with a standing desk and a computer; at the back of this ran a plexiglass wall closing off a narrow area that seemed to house some machinery and power outlets; wires ran from the computer through the plexi to a wad of cables on the floor. Nothing else. No doors or windows. He wanted to leave the door behind him open but it was heavy and probably self-closing; he considered taking off a shoe to prop it open, but instead he made his way to the computer terminal. Nothing. No mouse or keyboard. He realized the CPU was actually on the other side of the plexi and this was just the monitor and...he spotted a microphone and speakers built in to the screen.

He talked at it, "Hello, hello?"

Immediately, the monitor powered on. Simple text instructions appeared on a green background. *'During the following, say* One *to end the game. Say* Two *to go on to the next screen.'*

He felt his heart racing, and he said grimly, "Two."

The screen dissolved and new instructions appeared: *'Your choice indicates you would like to negotiate. Say* One *to send an automated warning message to the units closing in on this location. Say* Two *to end the game.'*

Grinding his teeth, he said, "One."

A long pause followed. An archaic cursor line blinked nervously. Pat clenched his jaw, angry. "Come on," he grumbled. Nothing. He was about to get to his feet when more text unfurled.

'You have saved the game.' Camel's jerking me around! Slowly, more text came. *'The game continues.'* Pat sighed out, surprised how afraid he had been. He knew the people up top had been jerking around Camel, too. Idiots! Everybody needs to calm down...

More text came. *'In this scenario, you will be asked five fact-based questions. Each question has three possible answers. CORRECT answers will be displayed at the end of the test along with your score. If you score less than 33%, you will be given access to a human helper for other parts of the game.'* He smirked. *'All data used for these questions is readily-available and taken from the following accredited sources: World Data, NOW, and Nobel. Are you ready to play? Say YES or NO.'*

He loosened his jaw enough to rasp, "Yes."

After a brief pause, the screen went blank. Was it slow on purpose to piss him off? The text populated a row at a time:

Question One. Approximately 8,300 metric tons of virgin plastic has been produced. How much of that plastic is still in the environment—33%, 50%, or more than 66%?'

He had no idea—how would he?—but he liked the threes: "Thirty three."

'Question Two. How long does it take plastic to decompose—50 years, 100 years, 450 years or more?'

He wanted to say '50' but he guessed this was not enough. "A hundred."

'Question Three. Estimates are there will be 10 billion people in the world in the year 2100. How many are there today—5 billion, 7 billion or 8 billion?'

He vaguely remembered something about the population doubling. "Five billion."

'Question Four. How many people in the world have some access to electricity?—25%, 50%, 80%?

Why was Camel asking questions about that? Something about scarcity and the Third World? But, at least, it was an easy one he remembered from school. "Fifty percent."

'Question Five. Global climate experts believe that over the next 50 years the average temperature will: Get Colder; Stay the Same; Get Warmer.'

He hesitated. Then he sighed: "Get Warmer."

The screen flashed his score:

'Your score is 20%. One CORRECT answer, Four INCORRECT Answers.'

Pat caught himself before he started swearing. More text:

'Question One. Approximately 8,300 metric tons of virgin plastic has been produced. **66%** *of it is still in the environment.*

'Question Two. It takes plastic **450 years or more** *to decompose—some scientists say it will never decompose.'*

'Question Three. There are 7 **billion** *people alive today'*

*'Question Four. **80%** of people in the world have some access to electricity.'*

*'Question Five. Global climate experts believe that over the next 50 years the average temperature will: **Get Warmer.'***

"That fourth question is a trick question." Did he say that aloud? Yep, he was talking to a machine. Or was he—was the Worm just keying this all in, making it up? Pat could feel his face burning. This was not only a trap, it was an exercise in humiliation.

More text:

'The good news is, you, and most people surveyed, got Question Five right. The bad news is, your score of 20% is worse than if you had guessed. Guessing, you would have averaged 33%. You will be given access to a human helper for other parts of the game. Say YES to continue. Say NO to end the game.'

Pat sat staring at the screen, raging, unwilling to answer, ready to punch someone. After a time, the text appeared again on the next line,

'Say YES to continue. Say NO to end the game.'

Were these real stats? If so, hell of a lot of plastic. Seven billion on the way to 10 billion—hell of a lot of people. How would these future folks deal with the heat? And how had so many people gotten electricity? That was hopeful, at least. He felt a strange surge of excitement and curiosity. Pointless trying to punish a machine—it was the Worm he would punish. Keep playing the game, he told himself.

Out loud, he said, "Sure, why not. Yes."

The screen dissolved and a series of distant klaxon sounds could be heard. This lasted about half a minute. Was this meant to frighten him? Or was the Worm under siege? Abruptly, the noises stopped. A new set of instructions appeared.

'You have chosen to continue. Please note—'

There was a pause and then the screen blinked off and back on. Blank! Pat scowled and wondered what kind of game this was.

The third generator bypassed the second when it hit tolerance. Swearing, the **Worm** shot into the operations area of the room. He zoomed over to the CPU and flipped the toggle, sweating, fuming. He became aware that Steadson had taken a step back and was glaring at him through the plexiglass. Would he try to shoot his way out? In his peripheral vision, however, the Worm could see that the governor had not reached for his sidearm; he was standing still, smirking.

"Trouble with the works?" came his amplified words.

The Worm adjusted his glasses on his moist nose and focused on the governor's well-dressed form—the same thick hair he had as a boy, now grey, the same slight lisp on the 's', the slight addition of an 'uh' vowel at the end of 'works'. He'd seen pictures of him, he'd seen him on television...but in person, even behind plexi, the Worm felt a burst of revulsion mixed with excitement. Here was his enemy, at last. He forced his voice to be neutral: "Heroes are attracted to trouble." The reboot finished. "Resume."

"Are we making a deal or playing games?" the Guv asked.

"Depends how you do," the Worm said and shot back out of the room.

"Resume," intoned the computer.

Pat ignored the audio warning from the computer: *'Sixty seconds.'*

He didn't like computers talking to him, or talking back—not at home to turn on the A/C, or turn off the lights, or any of that crap. Now that he'd seen his adversary, he wasn't as scared of him. And he wasn't in a mood to comply. It felt good to be on his knees studying the edges of the plexi wall and its thickness, testing it with his fingers, hands on the problem. He wasn't a test-taker or an action hero; he was a straight-up guy, a deal-maker, a get-it-doner, a leader. Good to see a sign of weakness in the enemy, at any rate. He knew where the Worm was hiding, now how to get at him? He tapped—thick, probably bullet-proof. It was built into the wall, so there was no peeling or squeezing through. Hard to tell if it was recent or the room had been fitted this way.

"Thirty seconds," the machine relayed mournfully.

He gave up on probing the barrier, rose, and returned to the timed message.

'For this scenario's set up, do you consider yourself beginning, intermediate, or advanced in your understanding of chemistry? For beginning, say One. For intermediate—'

"ONE," Pat bellowed, scratching under his collar, chuckling to himself that had been the easiest test question of his life. He loosened his collar.

*'What happens when hydrogen comes into contact with electricity? If the answer is **violently explodes**, say One. If the answer is **nothing**, say Two."*

Pat didn't know, though he assumed hydrogen should be left alone. He knew that the petrochemical complex was vast—more than a hundred square miles?—and was volatile (5,000 injured during the energy crisis sprang to mind). He knew even before the crisis the big boys kept getting slapped around by EPA for violations. And he'd saved Houston's ass by intervening and getting everyone to play nice. But throughout the crisis, he had categorically told his aides, his lawyers, his enemies, his allies, that he had no interest in anything but top-level info.

"I don't need to know squat about what you do or how you do it," he'd told the safety managers of Lyonn, Burning Water, Chuw and the rest, including Pythos, probably, though, he didn't remember all the names. "I need to know is you've done exactly what you've been told so I can stop the Feds shutting this whole city down."

And so here he was, and he didn't even really understand what hydrogen was. Dang, that's just stupid. It was a gas, it was in water, molecule, there was a lot of it. It was the name of the second round of atom bombs. Shoot. This question was being asked because it was deadly, right? Why else would they ask? Then he remembered the thunder and lightning storm outside; it clicked; the Worm had picked a night with lightning on purpose!

"One," he said confidently. "Violently explodes."

'Correct. Next Question. Lyonn of Houston has 50 hydrogen tanks. If one of them leaked, and the hydrogen gas came into contact with lighting, rate the scale of the damage from the explosion, using the Enhanced Fujita Scale: Light. Moderate. Considerable. Severe. Devastating. Incredible. Make only one selection.'

He'd heard of the scale on the weather forecast for tornados. He wasn't really sure what each meant—something to do with what buildings would get knocked down? He knew from the crisis days that even with all the flares and computers and fail-safes, this whole complex was a big old ticking bomb. He was conservative by nature, however, so he went with, "Severe."

'Your answer has a one percent chance of being correct. Make another selection.'

"Devastating," he said, annoyed.

'Your answer has a six percent chance of being correct. Make another selection.'

"Incredible."

'Your answer has a fifty-one percent chance of being correct.'

Incredible damage...the Worm sure knew how to scare him.

'Would you die for your country? Yes or No.'

Pat replied immediately, "Yes."

'Would you die for your planet? Yes or No.'

Pat hesitated. Where was this human helper he'd been warned about? He said scornfully, "This isn't a movie. You people and your pipe dreams. This is the real world, right here. And this is how we make things and get things done."

'Yes or No.'

"How you think you can stop the free world from doing business, Worm?"

'*Yes or No.*'

"You want me to tell White and Chuw and Shell and all these mega companies to stop using fossil fuels and making plastics...tomorrow? Otherwise, you blow up this plant? That's what this crackpot plan of yours is?"

'*Yes or No.*'

"My God, you're nuts, aren't you. You're crazy."

Insistently, like scolding a child, the machine's audio kicked out, "*You have 10 seconds to answer the question. Yes or No.*"

"NO!" Steadson bellowed.

The machine returned more text. '*The next scenario in the game is ethics. You will be given access to human assistance.*'

He noticed a hum. He looked up—Camel was back behind the plexi, in the wheelchair. The bastard's voice came out tinny through a speaker: "Die for your country but not your world? Wanting to save the world is crazy but wanting to destroy it is good business? Poor logic, Hero."

"Hey. Not much of a game, Worm, just pie in the sky."

"Isn't it more accurate to say 'hydrogen in the sky'?"

Pat went silent. Here it came, finally, the threat. He waited. Camel twisted around in his chair—a bit squeamish about violence? Maybe he could use that. "Let's be reasonable. Let's talk about—"

"No!" the other screamed. "You want to be UNreasonable. Your score so far is worse than a monkey who was simply guessing! How will you ever compete on the Ethics section? But maybe your Christian values can help you, Hero. Are your Christian morals worth anything if you actually follow them? What will you do for your country tonight since you don't care about the world?" He paused. "You have a granddaughter? What kind of country in what kind of world do you want for her? I don't have children. I'm not even a believer. And I care more about the world than you do."

Pat exploded, "What the hell do you think you're gonna accomplish?"

The Worm's eyes blinked and looked away; an odd duck. "You're the politician," the man mumbled. "What are you going to accomplish?"

"Go ask some liberal, not me," Pat declared with finality.

"Dem-Reps can't get anything done." Pat almost laughed; the Worm looked him in the eyes, almost pleading: "We need you, Governor." Not Hero, Governor. Hmm.

"This is nuts. You're full of crap." Pat almost spoke his name, decided against it. The guy wasn't a worm, he was a weasel. He was looking for an easy way out of whatever trap he'd made for himself; well, Pat wasn't into throwing away resources on charity. "Or else you blow up half of Houston? That's your threat? Why should I believe you can do it?"

"Please listen." Pat was astonished—the guy was pleading? "Survival is good for business, Governor. Disasters...not so much."

He felt his will firm up, like when negotiating. "I'm walkin' out of here if you don't talk sense."

"If you walk out, and an ethylene fire starts, we both die. If there are hydrogen leaks, and if lightning hits it, this plant blows and likely torches the one to the south because that's Chuw—you know, the dirty outfit you bailed out, the one with the worst pollution record in history? So it'll light up quick. If the fire spreads to Chuw, even with all the safety shut offs at every plant around, look out, flares and lightning mean more could go up until you got the equivalent of several hydrogen bombs." Pat felt his bowels churn. "Largest hazardous disaster in U.S. history. All thanks to you being deaf to facts and reason. But it could spark a debate for safety and environmental controls. Maybe usher in alternatives to plastic. Or maybe, just make a big mess in a world of messes. One thing's for sure, it'll get people's attention."

"This is all bluff."

"When it comes to ethics, there's no bluffing." And on that declaration, the Worm wheeled out. Pat jumped to his feet but was helpless to stop him.

The message on the computer screen blinked,

'Ethics. During this scenario, you will be given access to human assistance.'

Pat groaned and sat back down. Implacably, the monitor flashed,

'Scientists estimate that a 2-degree Celsius increase in average mean world temperature would be catastrophic. Climate change models predict this increase would lead to a collapse of the sea-based food chain and billions of dollars of damage to property because of sea-level rise, flooding, and wild fires. If no changes are made to current carbon emissions, predictions that this will occur are as high as 60%.'

Pat fumed. He didn't even know what the darn Celsius scale converted to. "This is America, talk to me in Fahrenheit, damn you," he demanded. On the screen, like magic, 'Two-degree Celsius' turned red and morphed into '3.6-degree Fahrenheit'. "That's better," he growled.

'To decrease the risk of catastrophe, you will be able simulate the effect of a percentage reduction in emissions by the year 2050. Choose one of the following reductions to attempt in the simulation: 5%, 25%, 60%.'

"Zero," he grumbled. Zero was not offered. So he thought for a while. What were the chances all this hullaballoo had legs? 2050. Leo would be 40—a mother herself probably. He supposed there might be some increase in temperature—he'd sure heard enough griping from farmers. But 3.6 degrees was panic talk. Have to take a number, take the lowball. "Five percent."

'Using 5% as a target for reduction, and assuming climate disaster is to be avoided at all costs, reduce U.S. emissions in the following simulator. The model assumes the same adjustments will be made in other

countries—' a game-like interface came up—'*Reduce U.S. industry, manufacturing, energy and transportation carbon emissions by 5%. At that point, the simulator total will display 0.*'

What followed was an interactive section which let Pat raise or lower different sources of energy, sequester more carbon (blue carbon?), impose restrictions on emissions. After some trial and error, he was able to do it. Painful here and there but doable. He was proud of himself. Then, ten different projection models formed and his solution was applied: the world economy collapsed in eight of them.

'*Would you like to try 25%? Or are you ethically satisfied with your strategy?*'

Two models were strong. Eight were in shards. It was just a game. It was rigged. Hell with it. "Yes," he said in a bored tone.

Twenty-five percent reduction took a lot of doing. He was hazy on 'blue carbon' but knew all about methane—so we all eat fewer steaks? He moved green production up, chose to develop something called 'ocean omni-turbine energy', lowered fossils, invested in electric infrastructure; he swapped materials; he boosted re-use, reduced recycling. He bumped up sequestration to keep down emissions. He remembered the pandemic before the energy crisis—they found a lot of unnecessary this and unnecessary that—he knew more about some of the measures. Finally, one more tweak—upped telecommuting and, wincing, electric car incentives, why not? This world looked very different. Other forms of energy besides fossils was the obvious trick to Camel's game. But anyway, it was possible. If the model was close to accurate. Dang. He submitted his strategy.

As in the 5% simulation, ten projection models came up. This time, the world economy collapsed in four of them. He stared at the six models still standing. Four out of 10 equaled disaster. Slightly better than 50/50.

'*A telephone call is being initiated to assist you in answering the following ethical question.*' Pat could hear a dial tone and then rapid-fire beeps. Meanwhile, the question ate up the screen: *Is climate disaster an ethical question? If it is, what percentage risk of climate disaster is justifiable?'*

Tanya was relieved when the car stopped in the garage, leaving the crazy rain and lightning behind. As the garage door descended, however, she spied umbrellas in the driveway, shielding two D-Rep bigs, a man and a woman. Automatically she clicked the opener and the garage door rolled back up. The big-drop rain drummed and bounced off their umbrellas. She vaguely knew their faces but couldn't recall their names, and, frankly she was too fried to care.

The man waved and hollered, "Senator, sorry to bother you, but—"

She interrupted curtly, "I'm late to get home to my daughter, not a good time, call me tomorrow."

"We've been messaging you...this Worm fellow has set you up as a resource to the Governor."

Tanya stopped cold. The man's face was pinched, the woman's blanched. They had remained outside the garage, their umbrellas like trampolines for the drops dancing off in every direction beneath the powerful security lights Will had insisted upon.

"Resource?" She glanced at her smart—it had blown up. She clicked off the screen and looked at the man and asked, "What are you talking about?"

"I know, it's...the Worm asked us to stand by in case Steadson needs ethical advice."

Tanya laughed out loud. Then she got angry, "You gave my phone number to a terrorist?"

"No, it's this smart." He held up a smart device. "Senator, please. You know Steadson's gone in to try and negotiate so the Worm won't blow up the Chuw petrochemical plant?"

The woman clarified, "Pythos."

"That one too."

Tanya stared at them; she could almost hear her eyes clicking—they were dry and blinking took effort, and breath flowed hot out of her nose. Lightning danced above the rooftops, emphasizing the surreality (Will's word) of a life in public service. She longed to retreat into her safe zone, the home he had set up to protect them from the 'job', also his word. She wanted to tuck in her daughter and tell her she loved her.

She spat, "What am I, Ethics for Morons?"

The woman nodded a bit, as if understanding. The man shrugged. "It's a kind of test or game this Worm is putting Steadson through. Apparently, that's the intel that came out of the briefing."

She spoke harshly. "The briefing, Steadson wouldn't let me in the briefing, and then they left me high and dry in that hotel. Are you sure whose game this is? Did you say an ethical game? Isn't Steadson a good Christian? What does he need me for?" She didn't try to keep the sarcasm out of her voice. The woman...René was it? Something like that. Imperceptibly shaking her head. Great, once again Tanya was being critiqued. She was pissed at all these fucking people...

"Senator," the guy said, "The Party feels this is an important bi-partisan moment."

"Excuse me? You the Party talking to me? What the hell does that mean, Jerry?" His name leapt onto her tongue as she was talking—she couldn't remember his last name but it was really long and hard to pronounce. He was probably the architect of the gag order. "What am I now, the conscience of Texas?"

"Kind of," the woman said. Not René, it was like that...Brinna?

"Isn't your name Brinna?"

"Corvata, we met at the Majority training."

Tanya waved that aside—another sacrifice she'd made that she suspected wasted her time. 'You're never going to let me be Majority Whip,' she thought. 'If we ever get Majority again.' Aloud, she announced, "I'm sick of this Party, it ain't no fun, I'm going home. My Nanny's about to kill me, I'm two hours late, good night."

"This could ring any time," Jerry said, holding up the smart like it was a scorpion and motivated to sting. "It's a great opportunity. For you and for...us."

Tanya made an unladylike noise, the kind her mother would have slanged her for. "Why am I the only one in the Party with *pelotas*?" She wide-eyed Jerry, but he just turned red. "So you know that word." Well, this was the way things were. She shrugged, "Yeah, and don't you forget it. I'm going inside."

The house was cool and it was a relief to shuck the broken wet shoes. Cherie was there in a moment, circles under her eyes but poised and, somehow, aware—probably from LNews—that things were all fucked up and, with a few words from Corvata who'd followed her in, Tanya found herself told not to worry or go into see Loo, Cherie would make sure she was asleep, and even though Tanya tried to object she found herself in the living room rubbing her cold toes, Jerry handing her a glass of whiskey. These fucking people. This, instead of snuggling with her kid. She took a long drink. Jerry kept holding the magic smart like he was afraid it would bite.

"Oh for God's sake, Jerry, put the damn thing down."

He put down the smart and crossed his legs, a bit primly. "Senator, I'm very sorry, this is just one of those things we run up against. Everyone feels—"

"I get it!" Tanya said impatiently. "I get it, oh my, all the feelings everybody feels. Jerked around, that's what Mr. Guv did to me tonight." She took another drink. She checked her smart—thirty messages, lord, what a night! Sure enough, she found Jerry Washelkowsky's message—okay, okay...this was the job...she had to do the job. She stared at Jerry. "Okay Jerry. Okay Jerry, what do you know about this call I might get?"

He sighed out and folded his arms. "Not much. Seems Steadson did something to this Worm and the guy wants him to atone. I gather he's...testing him. I wouldn't be surprised if the whole business is going to be broadcast somehow."

She felt that dreaded jolt at being publicly exposed; ever since the funeral. But her mind turned over what Steadson might be facing. "You mean like..." She grabbed for a legal analogy: "You mean like Steadson is being put on trial?"

"Well said."

"So the Big Whig goes on trial. For what?"

"Something to do with the petrochemical district."

"For reversing all the environmental legislation?"

"Possibly an unusual brand of eco-terrorism."

"I don't see how he can get away with it."

"I don't think he wants to," Jerry said. Tanya wondered if Dennis was sharing info with the Party before telling her. Then she checked herself—Dennis wasn't the only smart person digging around into this mess. Jerry went on, "I think Steadson's the bait and the victim."

"Mm-hmm. To do what exactly?"

"What do you think?"

"Mm-hmm." Tanya hoped Jerry didn't know she said this when she was unsure...bemusement followed—maybe I shouldn't hide when unsure. Why would I know what a couple of psycho men wanted to do besides measure swords? She sucked on the ice in the whisky glass and got a few more tingles of alcohol on her tongue. She badly wanted another drink but turned the tumbler over and put it down on the glass table: no more. She messed Dennis—'What new?' What was Dennis' word for The Worm's tactics? Demonstration?

Then she turned back to Jerry. "But if Steadson gets advice from me, he could spread the blame."

"Or the accolades."

Tanya guffawed. "You know I own one of those bumper stickers, 'Zero of Houston'. Never put it on. We're gonna help this hard-line tyrant? Can we save the situation and help him screw himself?" Tanya got up and paced around. "He hates every social issue from word go. Not to mention the toxic soup his partners made in the Gulf."

"We can't take chances, Senator. If a chunk of the petrochemical complex blows, thousands will die and the damage will be on par with the nuclear explosion in Hiroshima." Tanya felt the blood leave her face and almost lost her balance, putting a hand out against the table to steady herself. The horrifying images they showed her in school flashed up afresh...Hiroshima...

"So..." She swallowed, wishing she had that drink. "So we're sure this is..." Her voice wasn't steady. "So this is what this Worm wants to do? Why the test? Or the game?"

"We don't know. But let's do all we can to help. If Steadson calls, will you talk to him?"

"Why me? Because I identify black? I'm a woman? Easy to discredit, right?"

"You're the other perspective," Jerry said smoothly. She wasn't sure she hated him. He wasn't from Texas, he was from...where? Los Angeles or somewhere in California. In his shiny leather shoes. With his smug attitude.

"Don't like the sound of any of this."

She checked a return from Dennis: 'A demonstration is indicated. Steadson could find himself dealing with a feint retreat, which is another deception. Gut check, it's layered.'

Tanya whistled. This was outside her area of knowledge—she was a senator, not a game strategist! "Jerry, I need a minute. I want to see my daughter's okay. Follow me if you want." Jerry opened his mouth but stayed put.

She climbed up to Loo's bedroom. Outside, Cherie was whispering to whatever-her-name. "She's asleep, Mrs. Mack," Cherie said. The two women in the hallway seemed to have agreed not to let Tanya in, but she opened the door anyway. Loo's eyes were closed and her face looked peaceful, which relieved her...and then pissed her off because she was hoping to use her as an excuse to get away from these people. Instead, she shut the door.

"You can go home, Cherie, I owe you big time."

"No problem, I'll message in the morning."

They went back down. Jerry escorted Cherie to the front door, and the other woman hovered near the bar but didn't ask for a drink. "What would you do?" Tanya whispered. "What's your name again?"

"Corvata."

"Sorry, you'd think I'd remember that."

"It's a bit unusual," the woman said. They were close to the same age. Corvata had almost transparent skin and was probably a redhead in her youth—freckles, too, all over her face. So damn thin, too. No breasts at all.

Urgently, letting out the venom, Tanya whispered, "What would you do—hurry, Jerry'll be back any second, or his damn smart will ring and I'll be stuck playing conscience to the biggest chauvinist in Texas."

Corvata murmured, "Children." She pointed upwards toward the second floor. "Yours, mine, everybody's, that's who I think about in situations like this. Old folks. We're responsible for protecting them."

Tanya looked into her eyes, surprised, chastened. Corvata's eyes were pale-pale blue, almost colorless. My God, Tanya thought, this woman is so fair her people might be from Greenland or something. How did she end up so far south in Texas, land of the merciless sun? She must have to wear a hazmat suit to go outside.

"You got kids?" Tanya asked.

"Two girls."

Tanya nodded. But Jerry was back, saying something about sitting, so they sat around the glass coffee table, Jerry placing the smart not far from her empty glass. Tanya kept observing Corvata, arms folded and sitting erect, and she decided she liked her. Maybe Corvata was a big with a good heart (for once). Feeling mischievous, she asked, "So Corvata, so what do you think I shouldn't say if he calls?"

"Anything sarcastic," Jerry said mildly.

With acid, "Didn't ask you, Jerry, but boy you're an asset in a crisis."

"Mrs. Mack...may I call you Tanya?" Corvata asked.

"That's my name," Tanya said, aware of how bitter she sounded.

Corvata adjusted in her seat. "Imagine you're the man. Do you want revenge? If you do, why all the games? It's dangerous, it's complicated, plus you either die or go to jail. Or, do you want justice?"

"Go on," Tanya said, snapping her fingers, like she was talking to an intern. Why was she being such a bitch? She felt instant regret and waited for the backlash. But Corvata didn't go on. She just nodded slightly. "Well?" Tanya prompted.

At last, Corvata offered, "It's maybe something besides, or in addition to, revenge."

"Okay, fine," Tanya snapped. The whiskey had made her cranky! Shouldn't blame that. Was this the best the bigs could do? Justice, really? "Okay," came out more neutral, and Tanya took a breath and slowed down. "Okay, so, if the Worm is after justice, what justice could he hope to inflict...I mean gain against Pat Steadson?" She stood up. "Wait a minute." Her brain jumped, even as deeper breaths were smoothing bunched-up nerves. She started the role play. "No Corvata, I see how you're going. So I'll play. There I am, I'm the Worm, I've got Steadson by the balls. I've hated him for years. He fucked up my life. I'm stuck in a wheelchair. I can't...whatever—have kids, sex, whatever. But what if I care about...more than just myself. I care about...I live in a wheelchair. I care about the less-fortunate. I actually *care* about...the future. I'm really a good American and I see how messed up plastics and pollution made everything, and I'm terrified of climate disaster."

Jerry shrugged and nodded and shook his head all at once. "We can't really predict," Jerry said. "But you take the call, maybe we get on the inside."

"If I take the call," she intoned warningly, miffed he'd interrupted. She understood Jerry—how sick of being manipulated he was and losing ground to the Whigs. But Corvata was on the real track. Softly, she repeated to reinforce her choice, "If I take the call."

The bigs had switched their gazes away, as if sensing Tanya needed room, and she followed their eyes, watching the storm through the large picture window. Lightning forking. It was one of those storms that just kept going around in circles, dancing down to Galveston, hitting the Gulf, and then sashaying back and stomping on Houston.

"Well I gotta say I'm confused, Jerry," she said forcefully. She was watching the melting ice ooze from under her overturned glass but could also observe two faces snap in her direction. She was going to enjoy releasing some of the last year's frustration. "Con-fused. See I've been told to stay out of anything public. Isn't this gonna be very fucking public?" She made a big shape with her arms and dared them to answer. They didn't dare. "So now, Jerry, you're asking me to take this call and stick my face out? When I have been told to shut my mouth and hide my face?" She paused and leaned forward. "You know what this year's been like? I watch every step I take." She looked over at her shoes with the broken-off heels and pursed her lips. "Been ultra-careful and my tongue is pretty much perforated from biting it. Oo, so are you telling me my reputation rebuild is over with? Because I was clearly told the Party don't want no game changer, they want them some team-player. Like this all is some sport! Ooo, well give me a scholarship then. I been Mrs. Take It For the Team Mack." She pointed at the scorpion smart on the table. "So now you're begging me to talk to the enemy?" Jerry shifted to speak but she held up a hand. "No, Jerry. You are in my living room. This is my rant. And I ain't done. See, I don't got to answer your smart. Mine is silenced—see? You get the symbology? My smart is silent. Mute. Like me. 'Talk to Nobody, Mack.' Okay. For all I know, you signed the gag order, Jerry. Did you? For all I know, you're the asshole. Are you? For all I know, you hate me. Hey, I coulda done something while the Party kept sliding down, but instead—"

The smart rang. She took a breath but didn't move. "Senator," Jerry said, pointing. "Please."

"No, gracias," she said, pointing back. "I've been studying Spanish, you know."

Corvata looked even more pale than usual, her eyes like fading blossoms. Jerry dropped his hand and looked astonished. "But..." he broke off as the ringer sounded again.

Tanya pounced. "Take off the gag order." She was tempted to joke about not being able to talk anyway with a gag on, but the smart was ringing and Hiroshima images rose up suddenly and she felt a little sick. What a risk for others and the world!

"I don't have that authority," Jerry was saying. "This is a crisis!" His hand was waving and shaking as he said it, his face, directed at Corvata, a tragic mask of fear.

"Sure is," Tanya said after another ring, looking at Corvata and nodding to signal she knew who had the power. "Crisis means people gotta risk."

"We'll make it happen, Senator, I promise," Corvata interrupted, picking up the device and offering it. Oo, so she was the bigger of the bigs. She was one of the assholes who'd strapped on the gag.

Tanya nodded warningly, prayed this whole thing wouldn't poison her, grabbed the smart and announced, "Mack."

No answer. She almost choked, pressing the plastic thing tight to her ear, afraid she'd drop it. "Mack I said." What in the world had she done? All for a power play? Risking, risking, her daughter, little girls and boys, families, wildlife—wait, she heard a sharp intake of breath.

"Oh-ho-ho," Steadson's voice sounded faintly, "Shoulda known."

Pat was flabbergasted. What a rotten game! He said formally in the direction of the monitor, "This is Governor Steadson."

The speaker made sounds like his watermelon buddy talking. "Hello, Governor, how can I help?"

"For the record, is this U.S-enator Mack?"

"It is."

"I see." He wanted to declare that the Worm should be crushed underfoot for all his deviousness. Instead, he repeated, "I see." Feelings in turmoil, he opted for polite. "Thanks for taking my call. I'm involved in a...touchy negotiation. I've been forced to call you, not sure why it's you, if you take my meaning. My status is...well. Think rat in a maze."

"Yes, Governor? Are you in immediate danger?"

"No. However, the Worm thinks it's amusing to have me answer questions like I'm in a testing station, and one of the questions is rigged up, I guess, so the machine dialed you...well, I don't know why, but I am obliged to consult you."

"I'm here," she said

Condescending. He hated that. He was trapped, hell's bells! "Dang."

"Let's work together."

"Well, it's some kinda morality test, I know you got opinions about that."

Tanya was delighted he needed her help. But she put that petty feeling aside. 'Must think objectively. Lives are at stake—maybe mine and Loo's.' Aloud, she asked, "Oh I got opinions for sure, what do you need?"

"Don't get high and mighty, now."

She writhed, ignoring the looks from Jerry and Corvata. What would she do for Loo upstairs? Anything but kill, she thought. "I'm here. What's the question?"

"I'll read it to you." His voice held a slight sneer. *'Is climate disaster an ethical question? If it is, what percentage risk of climate disaster is justifiable?'*

"Interesting," she said without thinking.

"Not helpful," he grated.

She said flatly, "Well, you might start by considering if justice and ethics are functions of morality."

"Don't double-talk me, Senator, I'm trapped in a concrete bunker with a...with a man fingering the red button, you get me?" Now the voice was threatening, and as usual that made Tanya saucy.

"I'm just defining terms—I assume you're familiar with critical reasoning." She paused a moment to let the sting land. "I'd say, Governor, the Worm has put you in what is known as an ethical dilemma. Not a moral one. Morality is easy—you follow your moral code; cut and dried. No, I'd say this is the grey area of ethics, a specific dilemma without a simple answer. You get these sticky issues as governor from time to time, don't you?"

"Yes," he said, sounding pinched.

"You're supposed to play this question-answer game, right? or he blows up hydrogen tanks?" she asked. "Something like that?"

"Maybe. So far it's vague."

The feeling of delight returned; there was a German word for that precise feeling which she couldn't remember. Then, as before, her sense of responsibility returned. Maybe she was being tested, too—after all, why had the Worm chosen her? She was a native of Houston, maybe that was it. More likely, though, she was the other side of the coin. And the coin was the problem.

His voice sounded irritated, "So you don't have any brilliant ideas, Senator?" he asked.

"Games can be instructive."

"I'm not here for fun."

"Games aren't for fun, they're to learn." Slight pause.

"I don't like games." His voice was stubborn.

She thought, 'No, what you don't like is being out of control. And the unknown. The non-routine.' She said, "I want to help."

"I don't like terrorism, Senator, do you?"

She'd caught his irritation and made a chiding noise with her tongue and then responded, "I don't care what you don't like. We're both programmed. We forget to be ourselves sometimes."

"We're elected officials, holding a time bomb!"

"True."

"And he might light the fuse!"

"Then cut the bullshit and let's work together." Tanya heard Jerry and Corvata's intakes of breath. "If there's any chance we ruin the earth, and we know it, isn't that a big fucking ethical problem?"

"I don't see the point of this exercise."

Pat felt that swagger anger building and considered ending the call—he looked around to see if he could.

Mack's voice came back, "How much time you got to answer this question?"

"How should I know? There's not much entertainment in this game, I can tell you."

"No more bullshit, Governor." The woman's profane voice was cutting. "Don't forget we feel anger exactly the same. Jealousy, hate, love, pride. Same. We're both parents, aren't we. You don't corner the market. We are exactly the same where it counts. How much time?"

"Where it counts?" He retaliated, "And where is that, ma'am?" pricking her with some easy innuendo.

"Our twenty-some thousand genes, Governor."

Her answer startled him: genes? "What?" he asked involuntarily. She didn't answer. What was the time limit? Or was the Worm judging the whole conversation? Regardless, he wasn't dealing with the question at hand but couldn't see how this woman was of any use. "Ma'am, pardon me, you don't know what it's like to be me. Be a man.

Raise a family. Lose a wife. I work my butt off every day but I come home to an empty house. And if you think we are gonna all of a sudden think alike, you're not as smart as you make out to be."

"God you're a self-centered prick."

Her tongue could slap like a hand to the face. Bracing. He chuckled, and some of his anger dissipated. "Well, well."

"I do know about the empty house. Just so happens."

"Oh. Right. I apologize. And...what about your daughter?"

"I haven't seen her awake for more than five minutes since we got home. In D.C. it's late nights every night, we only get time on weekends."

Pat nodded in spite of himself. "I-I hear you," he stuttered, an automatic ploy for sensitive situations. He regretted it. He did hear her, dang.

"What's your granddaughter's name?"

"Leo."

"How old?"

"Ten."

"Maybe Leo's the answer. Think about Leo's life—the next 75 years—and her grandchildren—another 75 years—maybe you'll know what's justifiable."

He saw how she was trying to manipulate his feelings. He said coolly, "You forget, Senator, I know the sky isn't falling, and this is just a dumb game."

"Your pre-frontal cortex thinks you know. You may want to be rational, but you're not. Most of us aren't—cling to our old paradigm, cling to the familiar, and it feels good. But what about the other parts of your brain and your heart? Governor...Mr. Steadson...Pat. Listen to me. Forget morality. Rely on your basic human values. On your cooperative instincts. On Leo your granddaughter. Okay?"

Pat felt his chest getting tight...

Tanya wasn't sure if she'd pushed him too far; it was quiet on the other end. She realized that Corvata and Jerry were watching her, listening, probably messaging one-sided reports. What had the conversation achieved? Very little, probably. Still, she had made a vow to Willie: no matter what, she'd fight to save mother earth. 'You fight,' he said, his lips lazy from the pain meds. 'You fight for Loo. And you fight for you.' Why couldn't Steadson do that? Fight for his granddaughter? For his dead wife, who was zapping around like Willie, yes? Quick bright flashes of that whole quiet courageous man she would never embrace again. She blinked tears. Shook her head a little. She heard Steadson make a little grunt, and she started to formulate an apology when—the connection ended abruptly.

She held out the smart. Call ended. She explained what happened; Jerry took the smart and got busy seeing what was up. There was some techno-speak about the way the Worm was communicating when everyone in the world was trying to either jam his signals or make sure he wasn't telling petrochemical plants to shut down or blow up.

Tanya felt detached. This was bad. Dangerous game. The Worm wasn't reliable and neither was Steadson. No place for children. She had to get Loo away. D.C. was no good—everyone was on vacation. No. Ronnie, San Antonio—that was it. Loo could hang with her perfect twin cousins.

"Jerry?" she whispered in his ear. He was chatting with his people about the call. Would there be another? Or would the Worm and the Guv piss off each other and...BANG. She closed her eyes. She didn't want to play but she knew she had to. "I'm making some calls, okay?"

"Yeah, stay close, not sure what's going on yet."

"I don't want to miss anything."

"I'll let you know."

Tanya moved to a corner of the room and called her sister. "Ronnie. I have an emergency here, I gotta stay but I'm worried about Arrianna-Louise, gotta get her where she'll be looked after. Will you take her a few days?" Her sister's annoying response she brushed aside with, "There's a bad situation in Houston. I'm helping the Governor." Her sister's comments on the governor were amusing but untimely. "Ronnie, I'm putting her on the next flight, pick her up and take care of her until it's safe here, okay?" Her sister made some comment about the time. "Who cares what time it is? This is life and death! I need you!"

Her sister, a bit stolid and unfocused usually, responded with energy that if the situation was life and death, of course she would be a good auntie.

Corvata was hovering when Tanya ended the call.

"What can I do, Senator?" the woman asked.

Tanya was dialing Feebee's number. "I'm calling my aide. I need to get my little girl to San Antonio, next flight. My sister Ronnie will pick her up and take care of her."

"I'll drive her to the airport myself."

"Nice try." Asshole. "No, Jerry might need you here.—"Feebee? You're awake still?" Feebee sounded a bit out of breath. "Big favor. I need you to take Loo to San Antonio."

"When?"

"Now." A pause.

"I'll be there...in...25 minutes."

"Perfect, thanks."

Tanya disconnected, looked up at Corvata. The woman had just sent off a message. Their eyes met. Corvata said, "I like how you handled the call with Steadson. You're staying?"

"Of course I'm staying. I'm...the Worm's got his hooks in me, too."

"Hooks? Funny, thinking of a worm with..."

"Earthworms have tiny claw-like..." Tanya started to cry suddenly. Willie again, Willie and his facts. She felt the woman's hand on her shoulder. Damn, she wanted a man to do that. She wanted a man; she didn't need a man. She didn't need to know earthworm anatomy. But she...she...she shook her head. Patted Corvata's arm gratefully. "Thanks,

I gotta get Loo up and dressed. Maybe you can call the airlines, next ticket out, for one kid plus one adult? Feebee's name is on file." Corvata was nodding yes. "Tell Jerry if he needs me I'm in my daughter's room." Then she stopped and looked Corvata in the eyes. "I want proof the gag order's done. And if you or anyone ever tries to gag me again, I'll break you."

Pryor could only laugh. What else was there to do? This woman either was a con artist, had a rotten boss, had a terrible job, or two out of three. Feebee's bedroom ceiling was a wavy textured pattern and...not interesting to look at. He pulled his boxers over his dwindling erection and, for kicks, snapped the waistband.

"Sorry," he heard Feebee say from the bathroom—she was sorry? When he'd made quite a mess of her eye makeup, kissing her eyes like that, licking her cheeks...? She must have work to do in there.

"Honey, it's okay I said. I'm the sorry." Pryor pulled on his pants. His 'chap' pants, he called them. Some chaplain he was these days. His job wasn't terrible, but not what he wanted—very little spiritual, running errands and finding poor people to vote right. He considered himself a man of the Lord, not a campaign gopher. He replayed the hot woman in the bathroom completely naked and mashed up against his shirt and tie; why so exciting? Better forget about it for the moment. He squinted into the mirror and started over with the tie...carelessly...he took a breath and, remembering his uncle's coaching, patiently wrapped a double-Windsor knot.

There was a bit of sweat on his forehead. He knew Feebee stashed tissue boxes in every room of her apartment, but he didn't have to go far to find one to wipe his brow—on the dresser, amid ornate bottles and some little wooden box—a music box? He opened the lid...no, earrings, silver and gold. Her little stuff. All her little things and behaviors, new and fun. He closed the box, found another tissue, wiped his whole face. A single woman's bedroom for sure, not like his—free weights and chip wrappers. Got to stop with the processed. Keep pumping, don't lose the body disciplined at College Station. His breath smelled weird.

"Fee, you got a breath mint anywhere?"

"I have gum...or toothpaste."

"Gum, never could." He leaned into the bathroom. Feebee's skirt was straight again, a sensitive spot on his front teeth reminded him of its thick zipper...her skin was still glowing and she shot a quick aching look at him. His erection resumed and he knew he'd better exit. "Never, I'll start the car."

"Five minutes, Vernal." She pronounced his first name with such tenderness—was it some kind of pity? Or was she the real thing?

"I'll drive ya."

"Thanks, honey."

Pryor loved Feebee's car. Not like his shitty American commuter. No, no, it had all the extras and the leather seats were swank. He wasn't a car dog but the way this machine accelerated made him feel like a kid on a board, flying headlong down a 'walk or ricking a wall. He slid in and lounged in the driver's seat and powered on. First, he closed the moonroof; adjusted the side mirrors until they were just right; reprogrammed the driver seat, tilting it so his feet dug into the mat. He sucked his front teeth—oh that skirt zipper stunt!

In the rearview, he saw light spill in as Feebee opened the door to the garage. He admired the swing of her hips as she locked the door, turned and approached the passenger side. Something about this night felt like a prolonged mating ritual. When, when, when would she return so they could end the tease started in her bedroom? He suppressed a shudder; his body wasn't used to this prolongated business.

Feebee climbed in and he pushed the keyless and the car said 'hello'.

"Talk about unintended tantric." Feebee cooed in a soft voice.

"Oh honey, you and me both. Let's get this trip over with, so we can come back to heaven."

He clicked open the garage door, leaned over and gave her a light brush on the lips, sat forward, lowered the accelerator, and the car shot out into the stormy night.

Pat recalled the feeling he'd got riding big swells in Hawaii on vacation. Go up or dive under? Or ride the wave in? Risk getting pounded into the sand, churned around like in a washing machine and spat out and then splutter to the surface, sucking air, shoulders creased, head down, hands on knees, coughing and panting, nose dripping, salt stinging the eyes...that was what this felt like. Except he was dry, and his chest felt like it was being squeezed tighter and tighter.

No, he shook his head, no wave this time; a hoop to jump through. I'm the prize animal, the lion. The hoop sports flames, but it's for show, it won't burn me. It's a hoop, just get through it, deal with this dad-gum nutcase. He figured the Worm's computer screen wouldn't really give him a choice. After the call with Senator Mack, it had reverted to, *'Would you like to try 60%? Or are you ethically satisfied with your solution?'*

He resisted answering. He wondered what Mack would do in his place. How she would play the game, with all her talk of ethics...cooperative instincts....Who chooses what it is to do the right thing? Game, he locked onto that, that was the key: he considered the outrageous 60% number and...and the anger dwindled, he felt himself pulling back. What if he played just to win? Just that, win! That would be how he'd approach this hoop, this game. Win.

He took the 60% bet. The simulator set him up. His hands moved quickly, adjusting the categories. He was fluent now—the interface was easy, the colors simple to follow. Green was good; so was blue. Red was bad; so was black. Some of the images used were actual ones supplied by NASA. He snorted while he clicked. He upped sustainable food practices—why not? Let everybody eat cake. The dial inched above 30%. Leadership in green energy abroad—sure, why not, he liked to travel. The dial climbed. He realized he knew a lot of these concepts:

adopt California air quality standards in Texas. Sure, that state hasn't withered like everybody said it would; it's just middle-class taxes; it's just a game! The dial clicked up. Let the EPA enforce the Clean Water and Air—sure, blame the cost hikes on the EPA! Pollution taxes on emissions—hit the transportation sector hard—more telecommuting, fewer flights—whatever!

He finished up with serious tweaks to fossil fuels and petrochemicals. Waste cleanup increase, green this, green that, Green Manhattan 2. Recycle didn't do squat—fine, ratchet up reduce and re-use. A little more of this—it's just a game—more, more, okay, a little more...until the dial hit 60%. Bingo. He readied to press submit. But he realized he didn't have to stop there. He could do more. After all, 60% was just a number. Was 60% good enough for Leo?

He argued with himself. "Why not? Everything is a numbers game anyway." But another part of his brain countered, "You know that's not good enough. 60%, dang, it's not really dominating. What is? Be sure. Don't screw up. There's nowhere to go—there's not some other planet to colonize. This is it. Plus, this is just a game." His other brain part argued, "Well if you're gonna be a nervous Nellie, something in the 90s would be acceptable." There, it was out, he'd quantified what he could live with.

He reviewed each of his set ups and cranked them all to the max—even though he knew the solutions were unrealistic—but the needle wouldn't go past 68%. Not close to good enough. He started over. He made choices he thought were realistic in every area and ended at 47%. He started over again. This time, he really went after fossil fuels and petrochemicals. He switched all vehicles except military and aircraft to electric: up to 82%. Cut plastic production by 15%. The needle inched. He cut plastic 20% and 33% and 50%, finally by three-quarters...and the Worm's game hit 91%! He felt a surge of satisfaction.

It was a game, he reminded himself, and it was rigged. Were these numbers correlated to anything real? Who knew.

Ninety-one. His palms itched. He reviewed the choices, made a few tweaks. The number dropped back to 89%. All in all, the choices were actually viable by 2050. At least, he could imagine them happening. Even a bad simulation got him thinking about how much bang you got for your buck. What was necessary? He cut fossils in military reserves by half, and the total rounded to 92%. Seemed like a super good number. He hit 'submit' and watched the result.

All ten models stood and held together. He'd saved humanity and the planet. He'd won. The Hero of Houston and the World.

He heard a crinkle and realized his lips had parted—he must be smiling. He looked around—was he being watched? Likely. He considered asking the machine to print so he could keep his choices for reference but then he rolled his eyes—sham simulation anyway, a game, not the real world. Not gonna happen. Don't waste paper!

The screen had gone blank. No fanfare. He made a noise of disgust. With a humming noise, the plexi lowered; he could cross over! The door, which the Worm had previously used, opened. Pat barked, "Now what?" He repeated this a few times before accepting the obvious...and stepped into the other half of the room, expecting to get shocked or set off an alarm...nothing...he continued and peered through the doorway. A ramp angled downward. Lord, where was this nut sending him next?! He touched the sidearm through his suit jacket, comforted by the firm pressure. He descended the ramp.

Tiny lights outlined a long straight concrete decline with a 90-degree turn at the end. A steeper grade than it looked, and after about 50 paces his thighs tightened up and his feet hurt; wrong shoes. He stopped and stretched, his inner past boy-athlete reminding him what to do. He felt ashamed at the answer he'd submitted; he'd betrayed his party; no doubt the Worm would publicize it. Never give in to hysteria, even under duress, and yet he had. He stretched out his groin muscles one leg at a time. Duress, but still...what other choice was there? He could sell that.

He thought of Leo, and her face came into his mind wearing a respirator, her skull blotchy with skin cancer...he shook his head slightly—it was silly. Marta had the cancer...God. He shook it off, shook his shoulders, leaned low, and stretched his hamstrings. He wondered if up top there was any help he could draw upon. No doubt the Worm had figured out he was wearing a locator. They were deep underground, maybe with shielded ceilings and walls, who knew. This petrochemical complex was like something out of a sci fi—how many millions had it cost? What secrets was it hiding? Better not worry over the details—that had been his policy. Right?

Resolutely, Pat proceeded, his feet hurting but his legs loose and striding easily now. At the corner he slowed. More tiny lights, running up and around a rectangle ahead. Forward. A steel grey door blocked the way. It opened as he reached out with a hand to feel for a knob. It made a slight pneumatic sigh, although it was the thickest door he'd ever seen in his life—over a foot. To his surprise, beyond lay a maze of corridors, wires, pipes, machinery, blinking lights. A deafening staccato alarm sounded and cut out. Red down-light strobed along the ceiling, the origin of their beams hidden. He felt he was at the threshold of hell. A muscle under his eye pulsed and fired—twitch, twitch—he winked, he rubbed the twitch with a hand. What other choice was there? The twitching increased. If his is hell, he thought swallowing into a dry throat...it's my hell. He stood taller. He was ready to fight, and he stepped in and, once he'd got through, the massive door hissed, swung, and thudded.

Pryor looped around the goddam airport departure ring again...that's 14 times. He told off the music and the car got quiet. He gunned it toward the smeary bank of red taillights and, soon, he was crawling again past the drop off curb. The lightning had shifted off to the south but the fat drops fell as fast as the wipers could move them off. Who the hell were all these people flying out in the middle of the night? And how long did it take Feebee to put a little girl on a plane. Hadn't his brilliant argument made sense? Why fly to San Antonio? Assign a chaperone, the airlines would do it for First Class, and call your boss and explain. No need for you to go. Crazy. And he and Feeb could be back in paradise in less than an hour...!

And why the hell hadn't he parked? Service had gotten spotty. Several of his messages got hung up and Feebee hadn't answered. He dug his hand under his boxers and put everything back in order and sat up. The comfy soft leather was losing its charm. The car nudged forward a few feet. Whistles blew...flashlights flashed...if Feebee called now he'd be in position to pull over and scoop her up in two minutes...GPS said twenty-eight minutes back to her place...two minutes to get inside...a minute to pee...and no time to get that hot skirt off again and—his smart rang, finally!

He used the voice activation to answer. Feebee sounded stressed. "Vernal, I'm sorry, I've got to fly with her, she's—it's...I just have to. Flights are delayed because of the storm but doesn't sound like too long. Sleep at my place if you want, and use my car. Honey?"

He fumed, bit his finger. "Okay, honey, I got you."

"I'm so—"

"Me too. It's okay. Do what you gotta do. Keepin' kid safe, okay?"

"I will. I'll probably be back tomorrow, I'll call you."

"Yeah, I gotta work, you know. We got the event." He could hear her breathing—she'd begged him to find another job. She'd offered to find him one....Right now he wished she'd find another job, too. Maybe they both could do better.

"I'll leave your car at your place. Safe travs, okay?"

"Thanks, you're...I owe you somethin sweet."

"Now you're talkin," he grinned, lightening up with her. "Worth waiting a few days for, you know it."

"Bye."

"Bye Feeb."

He told the player to play something funky and crawled forward a few feet closer to the end of the jammed-up cars exiting the terminal area, wishing he could get out and run off his dammed energy instead of creeping back into town.

"I don't know why he agreed to meet that guy. You don't negotiate with terrorists." **Tanya** scrolled WP, her lip tensing up, but there was no Jerry to soothe her with a remark or a knowing smile. The picture of the Lieutenant Governor waving hovered slowly. Smarmy. She looked at her watch—almost 2:15 a.m. What was his boss doing now? Was he playing the Worm's game or calling in an airstrike? While the good old boys strategized their spin in a fancy back room at the Corral? When would this all blow up? She kept waiting for it as the crazy lightning cavorted outside the picture window.

She switched Weather Wide—a map and a talking head. Red warnings, quivering digital windsocks: 'Winds over a hundred miles an hour'...'lightning strikes', 'flights delayed'. Shit! She dug out her smart and called Feebee—what else could happen tonight?

Pat studied this new room and its unfamiliar objects—brightly-colored geometrical...forms? A blob-like reclining lion. Was it plastic furniture? Artwork? Garbage? Now what game was he playing? His mind, seeking a course through this surreal channel, foundered like it had been asked to count sand grains along the shore. He took a breath, glanced sideways. The objects reflected various facts, figures, and images—ahh, they were projections and some even produced low-volume voiceovers. Like a science museum. He looked around but there was no visible exit. In the middle of the room were two upright panels and a tray, like at airport security. He turned back and studied the door he'd entered with its pencil-thin outline; but he could find no doorknob or control pad or even indents. Great. A rat trap.

He had read torture accounts from the border security detachment. He knew what tactics worked on prisoners. Isolation; suspense. That was it, the Worm was a sadistic bastard. Pat leaned a shoulder against the door, folded his arms, and let his face go blank.

A few minutes later, he was surprised to see a door on the opposite wall swing out and the Worm himself wheel in. The door closed after a few seconds—he could just see its outline. He restrained a jibe or even a, "Huh." He kept still except his eyes, tracking the chair as it surged to the center of the room. The Worm had some kind of wooden box or bin in his lap.

"Please walk through this security device," the Worm instructed, indicating the upright panels.

Pat sauntered up, sure he was about to lose the gun. He thought that was for the best. The Worm was surely ahead of him; time to catch up. He drew the pistol and held it in his hand while he walked through, the device pinging as he did so. "I don't negotiate with anarchists," he said. The Worm pointed at a slot; Pat dumped the gun there and returned and walked through again—more pinging. He removed his belt, a money clip, even spitting on his finger to torturously twist off his wedding ring—all went into a small tray. Finally, the machine stopped pinging. However, when he reached for the tray it was gone.

"Hey, my property."

"You won't need it," the Worm said.

"Give me my wedding band!" His finger felt naked—that band hadn't been off since Marta died!

"You won't need it."

"Thief!" Pat accused. Should he attack him now? What was the Worm's hidden arsenal? A pathetic bastard in a wheelchair—couldn't he just strangle him? He shuddered—no, he thought. I can't strangle him. But I can beat him, I've done it before.

The Worm was saying, "You certainly have a lot of labels. Blamers do. Blame's not going to help you with the second half of the game,

Hero. And," he held up the treasured wedding band, "Getting sentimental won't either."

Feebee's car rang. Weird sound, like an alarm bell...huh... **Pryor** couldn't look around, traffic was stopping and starting and it was tight; the screen just said 'private'. He told the audio to answer and a woman's voice said, "Hello, am I talking to someone called Pryor?"

He was taken aback a second and then realized it must be the boss lady. "Yes, this is Chaplain Pryor."

"We haven't met, this is Senator Mack, I want to thank you for driving Feebee to the airport."

"My pleasure, ma'am."

"They just announced they won't let any planes take off. It may be hours or all night. High winds, maybe tornado velocity. Where are you?"

"Not far from the terminal."

"Would you do me a favor? Go back and pick her and my daughter up? I'd rather you than a cab. We'll get you something for your trouble."

"Oh, that's no...problem. I will."

"Be safe out there."

"Yes, ma'am."

"Thanks. Look forward to meeting you then, Pryor. Good bye."

"You're welcome, ma'am, bye."

What the fuck? He told the car to call Feebee...no answer. Nothing. Shit. At that moment, he saw an opening and peeled through it and out of the dense lanes back toward open road. He'd finally made it out of the snarl and he was supposed to turn go right back into the thickie shit for the terminal! The loop was half a mile ahead. He felt like going fast, swerving around other cars until he was alone in the left lane for the merge. The lightning streaks were lancing back north as if angry God was hanging over the Gulf and had puffed his cheeks to blow hard. He sighed and hit the exit and angled back toward the terminal. A shimmering white-blue kinky bolt struck the earth.

"You saved the world in a simulator, are you ready to save Houston for real?" the Worm asked in his shrill voice.

Pat kicked at one of the odd plastic displays. "Get on with it!" Still stewing over his wedding band and his helplessness in the face of the sadist...! Humiliation and rage wrestled for a few moments as his eyes, suddenly dry, blinked and focused on the Worm's homely face, head slightly tilted, body frail in the wheelchair next to the tray with his possessions. Frail-looking, he reminded himself, but deadly.

He said, "Well dang it, I already played your juvenile videogame upstairs."

"You surprised me," Camel answered. "But juvenile? Kicking a Pythos display artifact is juvenile, but calculating how to avoid climate disaster?"

"Doesn't mean anything."

"No?" He refused to answer. The Worm went on, "It's a software simulation. Same software recommended to your staff four years ago, remember? During what you called the 'Texian Energy Crisis'? That you 'saved' the state from? When you cut corporate taxes and eased safety regs?"

"You mean turned right instead of left? To hell with you, Camel."

Pat realized he'd forgotten to use the Worm name. Screw it, he didn't care. The man shook his head a little, chiding, "To hell with me?"

"This is utter and complete...paranoia. Your computer's rigged."

"Yes it is. It's rigged with scientific data from the real world and combined with sophisticated predictions. It's the same software you could have used for your big energy decisions. And didn't."

"I see why..." He almost admitted beating the tar out of him back when they were kids. "You're a..."

"I'm a Worm. Yes. Please use my name, Hero."

"If that's all you got, I'm done with this." Pat started for the door, not sure even in his own mind if he was bluffing or not.

The Worm squirmed around in the chair. Good, the guy was feeling uneasy. "Giving up?"

"And you're done, too."

"Remember, Hero, the software is available for a very reasonable price. The taxpayers will pay for it. Just like they paid for your incinerators that are covering west Texas and northern Mexico in dioxins? Where is the money going to come from to clean up the Rio Grande?"

Pat put his hands on his hips. "I've had enough of you." He set his jaw. "Open this thing up." The Worm didn't move. Pat felt his face heat up. Too early to bluff, dang. He hated this. He had to get out of here. Not through these thick doors; he'd have to brawl some more with this son of a gun. His hands shook. A threat now, he feared, would sound empty. He could feel his heart banging away in his ears, like someone had a finger in each one and kept flexing it, like some form of torture, making it hard to think straight. This was poker and his hand was weak. How long would it take to get across and grab him by the neck?

The whiny mouth moved. "I thought your simulator choices were interesting." He spun forward a bit, the motorized chair making no sound. "To be honest, you scored higher than I predicted. Bravo."

"Bravo hell."

"But will you actually do anything useful?" Pat wouldn't answer. "Well, time will tell. Speaking of time, half-time is over."

"You're a sick man," Pat said.

"I am sick!" the man confirmed with a shout. "I'm in pain. All day. Every day. Pain that never stops." Pat studied him. "Radiates out. My hand aches. My feet go cold. Then my neck locks up and I can't turn my head. I lie in bed and I can't turn over. I asked one of my doctors if I could supplement the morphine with a martini. 'Why not,' the guy said. I thought, at least, a martini is sociable. It's certainly not a cure. I have no life. Years since I went anywhere except work."

"I'm getting tired of your maudlin story."

"Tired is right. Pain makes me tired. So tired I go to sleep without taking off my clothes or brushing my teeth or feeding the cat or putting away the dishes. Of course, there's no real sleep. Doze a bit, then wide awake in the middle of the night."

Pat waited, steeling himself against the conclusion of the pathetic speech. But it didn't come. He checked a stirring of pity—the guy was still a sadist, don't give him anything, hold your ground! Worm's forehead sank into his hand; eyes behind the smeared lens frames were squeezed tight and the head seemed to shake on its own. Was it an act? Or was it the hell it looked and he described? There must be a way out—Pat's eyes roamed around the room. Nothing. He was trapped in a dungeon with a nut and a bomb was ticking somewhere, probably, he could feel it. Second half? Stay on the offensive, he thought. With an edge, he bragged, "Well I sleep good every night."

This provoked the Worm as if he'd poked him—the head lifted and the eyes fixed on his, unblinking. "Well then, Hero, I think it's time you did something about that leaking hydrogen tank."

"What?" Here we go—he steeled himself for the worst.

"Your 'marching orders' as I've heard it said." The whine left the man's voice, replaced by a slow drawl, "It's a storm of some scope out there. The door behind me accesses the rear of the property. Leads to a rundown residential area. You go see Sawdee Pete. You hear? Sawdee Pete. And tell him there is an unrecorded emergency leak at Number Six. And he'll know what to do." Pat blinked. The Worm shrugged. "Otherwise, you can just walk away and pray lightning doesn't strike and blow up Pythos and Chuw..." The frail cheeks filled and then he puffed out a small amount of air.

Pat wanted to punch those cheeks. He growled, "Salty Pete?"

"Saw-dee Pete." The Worm had put the tray holding Pat's possessions in his lap; Pat felt like he was being robbed. His hand shook, his gaze strafed the gun, belt, watch, wedding ring...the Worm cocked his head and seemed to study him. "You might be able to save

Houston from what is known in the safety business as a chain reactive explosion." Pat grunted. "Your smart won't work but you don't need it or a GPS. You don't call for help, or we won't need to wait for lightning to ignite the hydrogen. Yes? Cops aren't welcome in that neighborhood anyway. You ask for Sawdee Pete. Everyone knows him. Knock at any door, they'll tell you where he lives, it's not very far. He'll be able to shut down the leak. He's the failsafe person."

A single safety officer working—not even on site! Pat couldn't believe EPA was letting these companies get away with such negligence. He rubbed his thumb over his ring finger—it felt like a hole. "My wedding band..."

"If lightning doesn't strike before you get there. Better hurry. I have a sensitive weather app: this is the biggest mesoscale convective complex in Texas in 30 years. And here's a factoid: lightning strikes males more often than females." The Worm didn't exactly chuckle but gurgled. "My goodness, what will you do with all these new facts stuffed into your head?"

Pat stared at the broken man, his head stuck in that tilted position, unable to even walk and yet...he'd got the whip on the Governor, and Houston. Retribution for a school-yard fight. Revenge, justice, sadism, whatever. How much of all the information dump was bogus? Was the hydrogen leak bogus? Right now, did it matter? Should he get on his knees and beg? Is that what this guy wanted? Bile rose in the back of his throat and he spat. The Worm's hands moved and green lights flashed up and, behind him, the door he'd come through swung wide.

He took a last look at his ring, felt a twinge for Marta; wasn't the ring worth fighting for? He noticed Camel sneering at him—he realized he was tapping his ring finger. Petty nemesis bastard.

Pat forced himself to walk out. "Careful out there," Camel's voice followed from behind, "Downburst winds have already been clocked at over 190 kilometers per hour." The last he heard as he passed into a breezy, open-ended passage was, "Can you convert kilometers to miles, Hero...?"

Chapter 4: Out Into the Storm

Pryor had been driving Feebee's car fast and was only 10 kilometers from the airport terminal when traffic came to a standstill along a small rise. The wind was gusting, the rain falling so hard the car wipers were on full. Immediately in front of the car was a small commuter, a little girl's face pressed against the back window. She gave him a raspberry; he gave one back. She poked up her nose. He poked up his. Then, all at once, his hair stood on end. Without thought, he threw open the door and yelled, "Lightning strike, take cover," running and repeating/ shouting, faces staring out at him from cars, and then he was sliding down a bank into an impromptu creek from the water run-off. He pulled his feet out of the wet and sat knees together, hands off the ground, like his grandfather had taught him.

For a moment Pryor felt silly. It seemed no one heeded his warning except a middle-aged couple, who ducked down not far from him. Aghast, he realized everyone else had stayed in their cars. His hair crackled and he heard a loud pop followed by an explosion. Glittering shards flew down from the top of the embankment followed by a trio of cars tumbling-hurtling downhill and smashing to a halt in the creek. His hair sagged, burning oil assailed his nose, a horn blared continuously. He crawled back up the embankment. Feebee's car was unharmed; ahead was a gap because the car there was all crumpled and scorched, as if someone had turned the trunk into a hatchback. His brain jumped to, 'What happened to the white car with the little girl?'

Then he prayed, "Lord, let me find her." He rushed up to look in the mangled car—empty. Voices were screaming into the howling winds but nothing he could comprehend. Frantically he cast his eyes down, saw a smear of white—one of the cars that had fallen over the side! He slid down the embankment; first was a pickup on its side, the white car lay beyond it on its back. The couple he'd seen were running the other direction, and a guy was bawling near the pickup. Pryor skirted the water and touched the upside down white car—not too hot. It was a four-door sedan, the roof semi-compacted, windows broken but intact. He scrabbled away pieces of the rear window and detected a low sobbing. Like a diver, he lay on his belly, reached out his arms and, slowly, his ribs feeling raw, swam-squeezed his way inside, calling, "Take my hands!"

Slimy small tendrils brushed against him and he seized them and pulled. A face dashed with tears and terror lurched into view and he fell backwards onto the sodden ground. Someone appeared and disappeared, the girl snuggled up against him, and then there was another explosion—the pickup truck!—and blinding light. Pryor clawed up the slope, carrying the girl like a football under his arm, away from the truck fire. The wind howled down and pressed him back but he ducked his head low and trudged-fought his way up. The next thing he saw were feet and heard voices—thanking him, yelling at her, another explosion below. He was on his back now, looking into the pelting rain and the roiling clouds, his hoodie had collapsed over his face. He could just make out the little girl's face and a few words could be discerned but seemed disconnected—'agate', 'house', '9-1-1', 'bless'—and then he was nodding he was okay and they must have been her parents and must have been thanking him, and he got up, dazed, and they were hurrying out of view, maybe they'd gotten in someone else's car to go to the hospital? Traffic (unbelievably) was moving.

HONK!—he was almost run over; defensively, he staggered and tumbled through the door into Feebee's car, his soaked coat sagging. He propped himself up with the parking brake. More honking, headlights close, and without thinking and before he was rear-ended, he started the machine, numbly joining the exodus...a detour...'Airport Closed, Road Closed, Return to Houston.' He couldn't get back to Feebee.

The traffic blurred. He had to follow the cars and go the wrong way, back to Houston. He managed to leave Mack a message that he couldn't get to her. "Road Closed," he said along with some other incoherent words. Should he stop and try and walk to the terminal? The traffic sped up, stopped, and started again in the swirls of rain and the booms of thunder. He wondered if he'd had a concussion or just way too much adrenaline...

How had he ended up in this situation? They'd set him up with Feebee in the first place. They'd used him, like in horse-breeding or something. It was so wet and humid and...and he was crying, a waterfalling guilt cascading through his body and out his eyes. But he'd done one good thing, he'd saved that little girl! Praise God.

The detour at last dumped him on the highway.

A weird shock ran through his body: he remembered the app on his phone! Shit—they knew where he was! He signaled over to the shoulder. He peeled off the wet coat while the rain pounded the roof of the car—it sounded like cymbals crashing in a basement room. Everything was turning to water, inside and out. Blinking, he deleted their app off his smart. Yeah. He took a deep breath. He wouldn't be owned. Yeah. Feebee was a nice...she was...yes, she was hot, but she wasn't their beast, and neither was he. He started a prayer. "God, forgive me. I—"

But the smart pinged, interrupting. It was Malory, messaging: 'Report to the checkpoint, 24 hours a day.' Lord, they knew he'd deleted the app...!

Lightning and clouds flashed, rain fell, traffic surged.

"God, help me." He signaled and tried to get back on the road...

Em was attracted to Tuck's mixture of little boy and boss. But this triumphant demeanor felt odd tonight. Instead of the usual assertive, he was...split, and something unpleasant lurked on the other side of the divide, like rancid oil. Brushing her teeth and taking a shower hadn't cleared it. She had gotten cold in the towel, so she dropped it on the floor and slipped into bed and pulled the sheets over her head. She heard him murmuring or talking a while...then, he seemed to be asking her questions or setting up rules. She couldn't hear very well and, annoyed, she stuck her head out and said, "I can't hear you, come in here."

He appeared in the bedroom doorway, a clinking glass in hand brim-full of probably whiskey, not his usual drink. Usually he was beer or, at a bar, a gin and tonic. He drank and walked back and forth and gestured, rambling about how they had a good thing going and that he liked her. He stopped after this flattery, apparently expecting an answer.

She gave him one. "If you're so worked up, either get in bed or go away and let me sleep."

He smiled and put down the glass but then took a long time removing his tie and shirt. He was getting a belly, but she didn't mind that as much as the bitter anxiety in his voice, "Don't think we should keep doing this." Again, odd, like it was from the other camp—like he'd been warned not to let her distract him. Cufflinks clinked on the nightstand. "I have to get up early." Tie dropped on the floor. "Did you eat in the restaurant?" Belt dropped on the tie.

She didn't bother answering, though he repeated the question several times. He seemed shy to undress in front of her—she had sat up, knees up and breasts tucked against them, letting the warmth of the pillows against her shoulders counteract the chill from her damp hair. Finally, he stood on the far side of the bed in socks and boxer briefs, as if unwilling to concede the argument.

"Why won't you answer?" She kept breathing slowly and deeply, letting him get whatever poison it was out of his system. "Are you listening to me?"

"What I am doing is, I am waiting," she replied.

"Did you eat in the restaurant? I want to know!"

"You are not paying me a per diem," she scolded. "Take off your socks, you look weak."

He ripped off the socks and, frowning, crawled into the bed and put his belly against her cheek. "Hey, I had a rough day."

"Me too," she said, inching her cheek away from his skin. "Don't fight me, you know who'll win." She watched for him to accept the warning and he nodded and smiled. "I think you like to lose sometimes," she joked. She withheld touching him, waiting for him to relax.

Instead, he straddled her and she eased back and stared up at him. "But I like to be on top," he said in a playful tone. She let him pin her wrists. He leaned over and bit the sheets and pulled them down and she felt the cool air of the room on her entire body. He brought her hands to her sides and used his elbows to press open her legs. It wasn't rough yet just...strong. His tongue worked along her belly and progressed to her inner thighs. She felt sweat sprout over her lip as soon as his tongue reached her loins. Gradually, her control slipped away...and she was rewarded with a long, shuddering climax.

Before the pleasure had dissipated, however, he pulled her onto her knees and put her hands behind her back, and slipped in. The thuds got faster and faster and she climbed up another wave of pleasure. But approaching another climax, he suddenly vanished...she opened her eyes to see what was happening, he was groping around and—

"No-what-STOP!" she shouted and fortunately her hips were slippery and she wrenched from his grasp and left him face down on the wad of sheets. Somehow he had his belt and was going to tie up her hands. With a sharp blow she slapped his back and grabbed the robe and put it on. She pointed at him: "You were taking me to a second paradise and you ruined it."

He said something muffled and then looked at her, face red, eyes flashing, like murder. Red flag! Reflexively, she slipped her hand into the robe pocket and loaded the recording app.

Then his shoulders flexed like a big cat's stalking prey. His expression twisted into a grimacing smile. "Look what I gave you first."

"It was good," she acknowledged, "But you didn't ask. I say no. You're not tying me up."

"Baby, please, you look so good and tight."

"No." She was angry and scared.

"Take off that robe and get your ass back in bed."

"No," she said. He sank back, apparently defeated, and she went quickly to her suitcase.

"Em, come on, you lose your mind?"

She threw down the robe and put on her bra and blouse. "No, Tuck, I didn't lose my mind, you didn't ask."

"Come on, it's so good, you'll like it."

She put on her panties and pants and slammed the suitcase shut. "I won't like it 'cause I won't be here."

"Oh no you don't, you owe me."

Surprised, she saw he'd jumped up and blocked the door, the belt dangling in his hand. A weapon. She felt her heart squeezing in her chest and tried to keep her voice firm. "You lockin me in this room, Tuck? You gonna tie me up against my will? I'll press charges." She told herself to keep calm and keep getting dressed; she put on her footies.

"I paid for this room. We're finishing this."

She stifled the reflex to plead, letting the hidden arsenal give her confidence, saying clearly and loudly, "Are you threatening to rape me now? Rape's a crime, Tuck."

"Pleasure's not a crime, baby."

"No is no is no. If you force me, it's rape. I'll say it again: NO."

He was still erect, which creeped her out, but she'd been in trouble with guys before, and she concentrated on the recent coaching: 'Use sensory words,' was the advice. 'Let us see it and feel it.' "I refuse sex with you, Tuck, I don't care you have a hard on."

He was moving, she couldn't deliberate, she scrabbled for, found, and pressed the 'post' button.

"No games," he was saying and reaching—

"I just posted the audio!" she warned and held up her smart as if it were a shield.

He stopped dead. "What?"

"We're on record. My account. You touch me, it goes out to the entire world."

"Em. You're full of shit."

She put her finger on the side button of the smart, thankful that they had given her the ability to record not because she cared about a bribe—someone was paying for this shit!—but because it might protect her. Still, she wasn't sure what he'd do next; how much would she have to pay? Would he hit her? Rape her anyway? But his eyes blinked at the object and his erection wilted; he dropped the belt on the floor and sat on the bed, maybe about to cry. She slipped on her shoes and opened the bedroom door.

"This is what I get?" he asked. "For everything?" She looked back. He got up, arms wide. "Em, really?"

"I need to leave," she said.

He paced laterally and punched the wall, denting the sheetrock. She involuntarily flinched, her cheek bone remembering the last time a man struck her. Tuck was roving back and forth, back and forth, like he couldn't stand still, but she was afraid to try and get by him. What next?

A knock banged on the outside door, startling them both. Em felt trapped between Tuck and his cronies, but it was an opening, she seized it—she held out her smart. "I'm still recording," she warned, "And posting. Time for me to leave."

Tuck grabbed his clothes and started getting dressed, and she escaped to the sofa and secured her purse. She didn't care about the suitcase or her toiletries, just freedom, and she got near the door—another knock, but she was ready for it.

Clicking his own smart and looking at it he said, "Fuck. Get back in the bedroom."

"No, I'm leaving."

"Fuck. Em. Stick around a while. We gotta talk."

Emboldened, she said, "You gotta learn what 'no' means."

More knocking. Tuck, tucking in his shirt, grimaced. "This is all in your head. You—"

She said loudly, "Answer the door, honey!"

Swearing, he started, stopped, glowering at her but she continued to hold the smart out and finally he complied. A beaming bald guy was there, and Em wasted no time chirping, "Good night, see you later." Tuck opened his mouth but moved aside and didn't speak; Baldy gave way with a surprised expression and she hurried away down the hall toward the elevators, throat tight as she touched the button and whispered, "Gracias a Dios."

Don switched on his nonchalant vibe, even though he figured Chambers would perceive he was fired up. Have to keep him out of the bedroom so he didn't see what he'd done to the wall. "So? Is the Guv crying for help?"

"We need to monitor the situation. Something's come up. But first, was that your wife who left in a hurry?"

Don squinted. "Sure."

"For a guy who lies all the time you're not a very good liar."

Don was annoyed. At the first opportunity, he'd get a different party contact. "What are you talking about?"

Chambers had been poking around on his smart in the way that older people did, and he turned it and it flashed a web photo of the wife, talking to reporters. "Oh here's your wife. You're in the public eye, Tuck, so's your wife. How're you gonna keep this...lady friend...out of the public eye?"

"She's nobody."

"What did you say?"

"You heard me, Chambers, now leave it."

"Oh, no, no no no no no Tuck. I can't leave it. I need to know. I can smell it. I can see in your guilty face this lady is somebody. I got a sex-th sense." Don was reminded how much he disliked being hounded, like he was sheep or a duck.

"It's nothing."

"It's not nothing if you were doing something adulter-ette in that bedroom. Were you?"

"I know what I'm doing and you don't need to know."

"Oh you think so? Well. Well this brings me back to what we were discussing previously, doesn't it. The fact you aren't divorced. The fact you're in the public eye. The fact that the lady friend is a...let me guess: a whore."

"Nobody cares! Nobody! Go ahead, spread the word, she can spread the word, I dare you, I dare her! My cohort won't give a shit, Chambers, now get off my ass or I'll...."

"Oh now-now, Tuck. Well and good, go on. This is it, partner, my ears are open. Tell me what you'll do. Give me the threat straight. I can take it. I'd like to know where you stand."

"Why'd you come up here?" Don demanded, irritated.

"Why? You want to treat this as a normal occurrence, then? A married man and a whore in a hotel room? Does the whore not have a mouth? Does she not have a socialist media presence? You want to treat your moral standing like it oh so don't matter?"

"Chambers, by God...."

"Yes, Tuck? I'm waiting. My ears are open. I'm in suspense. Here we are in your hotel room while a terrorist gets ready to blow up half of Houston, with nothing to do but get a line on each other."

"I don't want to get a line on you," he scowled. "I'm tired, now get on with it or get out."

Chambers laughed, a creaking sound, and then sat down in the chair Em had occupied earlier. Don felt a reflux gurgle in his throat, revolted at the difference—as if the exchange of Em for Chambers forced him to think of Chambers sexually. His patchy white and red face, grey stubble, fleshy jowls, bent nose, the idea of how he must grunt while in the act...a shudder worked through him before he could repress it.

Chambers was staring, studying him, an almost-smile on his ugly toad face. It was a stupid game! So locker room! But he had to play. Sighing, making sure the man knew how put out he was, Don sat down at the small table as far as possible from his adversary. He crossed his legs but Chambers made no move and the almost-smile waned and a frowning silence followed. The space between them reminded him of staleness—unaired rooms, bus terminals, dried out crackers.

Don waved a hand impatiently, "Let's get this over with. It's been a long day."

"Long day? It's going to be a long night," Chambers chirped.

"Like I said..."

"A long year."

Don felt his eyes narrow. Did he mean the run up to election? He hated this bastard, this bullfrog who sucked up all the oxygen in the room.

"I'm waiting."

"Storm's getting worse," Chambers said in a suggestive tone. "Keep breaking records, don't we."

"Records?"

"Drought. Floods. Hurricanes. You better get a line on it, they'll kill you."

"I'm waiting to hear something I care about," Don scoffed.

"Careful. Watch out you vilify when you don't understand." Chambers paused. "So in general you take the passive approach?"

Don squirmed but didn't answer.

"Not to mention hospitality. You didn't offer me a drink." The ugly man's voice had gone flat.

"No," Don replied tightly.

 CONNOR KERNS

"You need a makeover." Chambers poked his smart and then his head snapped up, tilted, nasty grin returning to his features. Don felt his heart rate jump.

"What happened?"

Chambers took a measured breath and in a low voice intoned, "Don't worry, just a shot across the bow."

Don got the hint. "What'd that bitch say?"

"I think just enough to end your marriage for good."

Don grasped Chambers' smart and looked at an anonymous posting next to a thumbnail photo of himself at the last convention. Caption: 'Look whose Sodom and Gomorrah party I'm not going to.'

Don put down the smart. Chambers was at the bar, mixing. "Never thought much of fetishes myself. I know J.J. wouldn't. Neither would the voter base." Chambers took a sip.

Don swallowed all the saliva that had flooded his mouth. Maybe that would be it. Maybe Don should call his lawyer to deal with her. How much was this gonna cost? Should he wait to see if she did anything else? Was it really just a warning? Or public blackmail? Was it really the end of his marriage forever?

"Want a drink, Tuck?" The wind rattled the windows and rain harshed against them. A great night, and a shitty night. Don's feelings were so churned up he couldn't answer. After a few seconds, Chambers purred, "Right okay, Tuck. Right, let's talk terror."

Pryor knocked on the door. He felt wiped out, unsure if he was still in some kind of shock from saving the little girl. But he wasn't afraid to face Malory at the 'Checkpoint'—a strange name for a block of rented rooms at the downtown apartment building. The quick prayer had gotten his feet back on the ground, if only he wasn't feeling so fatigued....

It took a long time at door 45, but Mr. Malory himself answered, calling out an overblown, 'HELLO'.

Someone else was inside—a hulking sitting figure who shrank into an average middle-aged guy when he stood up. Pryor recognized him as a local boss. "Hey, Artie!" Malory announced in a false-sounding voice, "Here's another Aggie. Hey, there, bud, you look like you been swimming."

Pryor felt his face twisting up. "No, not swimming, Mr. Malory."

"Just Malory, man. Christ, what a night. Having technology problems? What, from the storm?"

Pryor couldn't take the overload of energy any longer and blurted out, "No, I just saved a little girl, Mr. Malory." Pryor's legs trembled—okay, that felt good to get it out, but he was post-adrenalized or something. And scared, face it, stop denying. Just try and stand still, get back to that grounding from the prayer. Why was Malory still smiling, looking over at Artie, grim-faced. The situation here was unreal. Pryor continued, "I...I was...I took my girlfriend to the airport..."

"Ah, good, that's what we want." Malory nodded at Artie. "Mack's piece of ass-istant." He nudged Pryor, "Not a bad ass-ignment, eh bud?" Then Malory was back to Artie in a more triumphant tone, "I told you my boy Pryor was promise—on it for a month, I bet he's already got her in the sack. She a good little lay?"

"I just saved a little girl's life," Pryor reiterated. He moved past Malory into the room, not looking at either man. "And there was a lightning strike. Traffic stacked up." Pryor's legs were quivering, he could feel them both staring at him, but all he could see were the explosions and shouts replaying in his mind.

Artie's voice was demanding: "What is all this?"

Malory's voice quickly, "Get to the point, bud. What'd you find out about Mack? We got a big day tomorrow, making some big plans—can you help us out?"

Pryor flexed his thighs so hard he could hardly think, but it didn't keep them shaking. Where had his primetime confidence gone? He realized his eyes were closed. He opened them and turned and looked at Malory, thinking, 'You don't care.' He looked at Artie. 'Neither do you. I saved a little girl's life, and you don't care. And you think she's a black girl, so you really don't care. You don't care about me. Feebee and Senator Mack are targets on your board. Half of Houston could explode and you wouldn't care as long as you could blame someone else.' This came clear to him—why hadn't it before?

Because these were supposed to be his people. Pryor's mind jumped back to when he joined the Whigs Club on campus. Tee Four and Bradon and Cal...where would he be without those guys? They knew when to take the car keys away and pull him off the keg; to introduce him to Tina—it wasn't their fault she broke his heart; to steer him back to his academic advisor after the disastrous econ. exam; to hang with him while the vet put down Leila. Okay, those guys were his people. These guys...nah. What now? How do I get out of this? Gonna lose my job! Supposed to be a chaplain, not a party pimp!

His mind kept jumping around until it finally jumped up to God for a quick prayer. Then a breath. Finally, he just said, "I can't."

"Can't what?" Artie asked. "Can't WHAT?" he shouted.

"Now, now, easy does it," Malory interjected. "You're quite a character, Pryor. What's on your mind, bud? We're all friends here. You need a drink?"

'How about a towel,' Pryor thought. Chaplain, I'm a chaplain. We're doing God's work, we just sometimes...sometimes it's the devil you know...

"Sit down a minute," Malory suggested and proceeded to pour out some whiskey and handed Pryor the tumbler. "Artie's not good with manners, but we're working on him." Pryor sensed the tension between them—Artie was forcing a smile but his teeth made it look like he wanted to bite. What were these guys cooking up in here? It smelled like booze and stale farts—were these guys gay? Mobsters? "You've had a rough night, tell us about it."

Pryor looked at the glass in his hand, amazed he had taken it instead of recoiling. The term 'bad scene' came to mind, with the devil in his glass and two more devils in the room. He could barely keep his nerves under control, the whiskey looked so good, like liquid gold, signaling the bribes these men would pay to make him talk. He was stuck to the spot with the glass in hand. Artie hadn't moved either, but Malory was sitting casually, sipping, legs crossed. Where was the cross? Pryor stuck his free hand inside his jacket at his neck, felt the cold metal...gasped a little...and his legs stopped shaking and carried him over to a side table. The glass was extended in his hand but he didn't put it down. It was like he couldn't control all parts of his body at the same time.

Artie snorted, as if to say, 'What the hell's wrong with this guy?'

Slowly, Pryor put the glass down on the table. "Bless me, I'm done in."

But before he could move or say 'good night', Artie was beside him, hand on his shoulder, fake-friendly. "Listen. If it's party business, tell us. You got to."

Pryor's feet pushed the rest of him up, making him taller than Artie, and the man's hand slid off and slowly tensed into a fist. Pryor repressed a wince—a fight would not be a good idea. But he kept his voice firm: "I'm a Chaplain. I do God's business."

Leaning forward across the room, Malory said loudly, "Hey Pryor, relax, come on, sit down, man, none of this is a big deal—"

Pryor cut him off, "Good night."

Malory was up, his arms open, conciliatory, while Artie hovered with the clenched fist. "We'll talk tomorrow at the Meeting, okay?"

"Good night," Pryor said again, turned his back on the danger, and let himself out. Waiting at the elevator, he expected the men to come after him and hurt him. He pressed the button and stared at the door but it didn't open; when it arrived, he got in...and shivered, his upper body bouncing up and down. He almost cried and laughed but did neither. Instead of Lobby he punched Floor 2. When the doors opened he got out, he scratched the back of his neck as he hurried down the empty low-lit hallway, looking for the stairs. A fugitive. He ducked under the red exit sign into the stairwell. It was concrete and echoed as he clambered down. He slowed, took the stairs carefully, scratching his head again. He nudged the door open at the bottom. A long hallway led back to the lobby but an outer door loomed a few steps away and he pushed through that. The wind swirled into this corner of the building and he oriented himself—to the left should be the front foyer and the lot where he'd parked Feebee's car, to the right the busy street. He crouched and peered left...a guy in a suit leaning against the driver-side door! Lord have Mercy! Shit!

Pryor referenced Artie's look—disdainful with hidden suspicion. The clenched fist didn't punch but he was still reaching to get out from Pryor anything he knew. Pryor hadn't fooled Artie—he knew Pryor was quitting! Wait, he'd quit? Quit what, his job? Quit the party? God, give me strength.

Now what? The little girl's face appeared as he rocked back and forth on the balls of his feet in that windy porch of the fancy apartment building. He could stride over to Feebee's car, let the suit escort him back upstairs, and make a coherent report. Play their game. But he was pissed that these devils had jerked him into some kind of traitor game and turned him into a fugitive! Time to run, run, run.

Still crouching, he moved low out of the corner and into the rear lot. He wasn't sure what he'd do, when he heard an electric motorcycle start up. Without thought, he waved and ran forward, maybe expecting by coincidence or providence that it would be someone from the Christian Motorcycle Club he'd visited during last year's campaign. The rider wore nothing identifying creed or race or color, and the face was hidden behind a dark visor, and yet Pryor waved again. The rider's head turned. Pryor stopped a dozen paces away and gave a small helpless gesture; the rider whirled the machine, stopping beside him. Pryor paused and then saw, flashing around the corner of the Checkpoint, navy blue—two men, dashing into the rear lot. He straddled the rear seat and suddenly the two-wheeler's tires squealed; out they shot leaving behind the parking lot and the devils, not stopping for traffic. After this maneuver, vice-like the rider gripped Pryor's wrist and set his hand on their flank; Pryor did the same with his other hand, finding hooks like handles to hold onto, and he held tight as the quiet, powerful machine, after idling briefly at the stop-light, sped away, split two cars, and outstripped every other car until they were flying alone on the rain-battered street.

Pryor had been on the back of a bike once—a friend during Spring Break terrified him in Pecos. Here, in Houston, he was in God's hands. Fortunately, they had surely eluded anyone meaning to follow. "Hey," Pryor called out to the anonymous rider. But the rider tapped his helmet and thumbed back. Pryor called hey a few more times before realizing even on an electric motorcycle people communicated by headset; he found a helmet behind him, unclipped it, and put it on. By that time they had stopped at another light.

"Where to, *Amigo*?" a deep musical voice asked in the helmet speaker. "This wind is bad for the ride."

Pryor had not known it would be a Latino. The pious part of him calculated that most Latinos were God-fearing. "Amen and bless you for getting me out of there." The rider seemed to shrug slightly. "I'm not a criminal, I was just..." He changed his mind. "You can drop me anywhere."

But at that moment, a grey BMW cut in front of them from the facing left turn lane. Reinforcements!

"*Vamos*," the voice said and once again the bike unexpectedly accelerated, taking a right angle to the Beemer, slipping around its rear panel and then forward against the light. Fortunately, this late and this stormy, few cars were to be seen. The Beemer cornered and fell in neatly behind them, its blue-white headlights blurring angrily through the helmet's visor. Pryor untwisted his neck, his view mostly blocked by the bulky rider's black coat. As he clutched the anonymous Good Samaritan, they bumped over a divider, and he wondered if the electric bike could outrun a Beemer? And if the Beemer caught them, what would the party boys think and do to them? Would they think Pryor planned to defect all along? That Feebee had turned him? Strip him of his Chaplaincy? Beat up this innocent Latino? Did the party people actually order violence? It was another example of how naive he was. "Help me Lord," he muttered, forgetting until after he'd said it that he was mic'd up.

The driver accelerated across a store parking lot and out onto a side street, the Beemer following, aping them move for move. Pryor's mind jumped back to his plight. Did he love Feebee? Did he care about politics? Was this lashing wind and rain storm the apocalypse? His thoughts flew as erratic and fast as the bike dodging down a residential street. A 'No Outlet' sign flew by. The Beemer stuck close behind. Red and white concrete piers sped nearer, and he knew they were trapped. This street had been blocked off into a bicycles-only route. For motor vehicles, it was a dead end. The Beemer, sensing this, had slowed slightly—it was the reckoning. Pryor organized his excuses and chose a few tactics—indignation first, penitence second, stoicism third. But the bike didn't slow.

"What you doing?!!" Pryor screamed.

"Get skinny, *Hermano*," the voice in the helmet said.

Pryor squeezed his arms against his ribs and sucked in his gut and crushed his legs to the chassis and they *fricked* between two sets of concrete posts, so smooth, and at once they were through! And onto a paved street. He could scarcely believe it—no gouges, chipped bones or clipped limbs. The bike raced on, leaping onto a sidewalk and lurching down a side street—all the businesses were dark—Pryor now was lost. In God's hands, he thought, closing his eyes, hands numb from hanging tight. When he looked again as if by the whirligigs of magic, they were on a wide street—in fact, gunning past the apartment building where he started!

"Around the block—my car," Pryor belted out, sensation returning.

"You crazy, man," the voice lilted but the bike dipped, dipped again, aimed for the sidewalk.

"God bless you!" Pryor said.

He staggered off the bike, and splashed over to Feebee's car reflecting blue pricks of light; the suit was nowhere in sight. Pryor slid in to the cool interior, and fired the engine. The biker was already rocketing into the gloom—was the helmet shaking side to side, as if to say, "Definitely crazy"?

Pryor put his head down and depressed the accelerator, turning in the opposite direction, toward the Senator's house, hands shaking on the soft leather steering wheel. He checked the rearview...the only pursuer was forked lightning.

Pat paused in front of the first residence he came to. He was surprised how regular the house and the neighborhood looked. And the cars—he had expected...he wasn't sure...what did Houston's so-called Cancer Alley look like? (He hated these hyperbolic names!) Falling down garages, sagging roofs, gravel, garbage? But through the wild wind and rain, there was a large, new SUV; a jacked pickup truck across the street, albeit parked crooked up on uneven ground; across the way was a vintage Dodge in a carport, its faded seafoam paint glowing under the scattered light from the streetlamp. Some of the houses were small, some regular. Mailboxes on the porches, compressors in narrow side yards, garbage cans at the ends of driveways...could be anywhere in America. And yet, he had only run a few hundred yards from Pythos, a massive, supercharged factory...or bomb.

The boom of thunder and huge drops raining down brought him back to his dilemma, and he realized he was soaked. To the southwest he saw approaching lightning flashes. As the Worm had promised, the wind was gusting hard. He felt silly knocking on doors, but what else could he do? He spied a small white house with an ornate iron cross over its porch with a flickering light inside—a television? He mounted the porch and perceived through the drapes the outline of a wall-sized television. He rapped loudly. An ominous distant clunk inside answered. Without warning the door opened a crack and all he could see was a rifle barrel.

He refused to be intimidated and bellowed over the whining wind, "I'm looking for Salty Pete. Emergency."

A pause; the barrel wavered. A low drawl, rather polite, answered, "Big hos', next block."

"Thanks."

Heart pounding from the confrontation with the gun, Pat stumbled off the porch, the wind almost knocking him sideways as he gained the road. He turned his back to the wind and it shoved him through the intersection. The big house had to be the first one, he thought, set far back, with a smaller house in front of it. A flag lot they called it. He started up the driveway and, as if the word were out, a porch light came on. He could see a shadowy face at the window. Aiming another gun?

He stopped and called out, "Salty Pete?" The shadowy face didn't move. He cupped his hands around his mouth and shouted louder, drawling the vowels out, "Saawdeeee Peeete?" He made a big gesture at the big house. The figure disappeared. He didn't wait for confirmation, he continued at a jog, just like he did four mornings a week on the indoor track. He was in shape, he was even a bit glad, the running was welcome after the cramped underground and the computer monitor, and the smell of his own fearful sweat. Here he sensed the electric-y-wet storm humidity, and salt.

'Salty Pete,' he thought, what a name.

He had gotten around a berm and saw that the driveway arced in front and to the other side of the big house, which by his standards wasn't all that big. He mounted the porch steps, the railing almost giving way beneath his weight when a sudden blast jostled him. Then, the tail wind died and was replaced by a powerful downdraft, pressing him into a crouch. He crawled up the steps and through mud and something gritty until he could feel the bottom of the front door. The rain sounded like hundreds of faces being slapped.

There was no welcome mat. He probed upward—no doorbell. On his knees, he pounded on the door. He pounded more. The wind swirled; the timbers were groaning and he found himself clinging to the doorframe. He sponged off his face using his sleeve. He pounded again. As he waited, a crash of hail fell and fine white balls bounced around him. He shivered—was it the apocalypse? He pounded more and called out, "Saawdee Pete?"

The door opened a foot. A voice inside, a woman's voice maybe, though it was pitched low. "Ain't locked."

Pat hauled himself to his feet, opened the door, and leaned inside.

Naurain chewed harder on the bittern—she was suspicious. She had seen about every crazy visitor at Sawdee Pete's house over the years. But never a pink city man out of a crazy storm wearing a fancy suit spattered with mud, like he'd fallen in Buffalo Bayou on his way over. She didn't smell liquor. She chewed and chewed and swallowed. Maybe he wasn't crazy. She dug into the brown bag and grabbed another sweet and popped it in her mouth before asking, "Who you?"

"I'm the Governor."

Or maybe he was crazy. "Hey what?"

"The Governor. Of the State."

"Buss me a sheep," she grumbled, feeling a flash of heat and wondering if the bitter sweets were to blame. She put the bag down and folded her arms and stared at the visitor like he was crazy, which he probably was. She gave him her best annoyed look.

Then he made a lot of noisy demands and threats, but she'd heard that kind of thing plenty before. She reached over to the coat rack, grasped the rag she used for the dog's paws, and stuck it near his face. That shut him up. As if she knew she was lending out her rag, the dog growled behind the parlor door and she yelled until it shut up. The pink man wiped his face, which made it pinker, and then he started in on demanding to see Pete again.

Naurain had perfected a gesture, which worked every time, to get control of customers, especially men: she extended her arm and held up a hand, let her eyelids close halfway while shaking her head once and saying, "Don't cough me no nonsense." She held up one finger. "That's first." Surprisingly, he just handed her the rag and strode by, making for the kitchen. She called out 'first' several more times but he went right through the swinging door; before she could follow, he swung out again, and went toward the parlor as if she weren't there. Eventually he would find Pete's door (locked), but still, this wasn't the way, he had to go through her first, he had to satisfy her first, he had to pay his due!

"She bites!" This warning made him stop short at the parlor door, and Pogo growled again. Naurain folded her arms and smiled. "Anyway, ain't nobody sees Pete till they seen me," she said firmly.

The man had been desperate when he came in, disoriented-like, in a rush. But now he seemed to gather up all his man-power and aim it at her. "Ma'am, there's an emergency at the plant, and if Pete doesn't come fix it right away, we're going to die."

Huh? 'Scuse me? Should she believe this? She grew more alert. He had a rumbly, confident voice; he had a tough eye. But Pete had that machine that told him what was what; so she figured it was a lie.

"What you gonna give me take you to Pete?" she asked, in her sweet baby voice.

He said, "Take whatever you want." He held out his arms. He pulled out his pockets—nothing. She felt a bit shy, but she stepped forward and, keeping her face away from his body, she felt around...no belt. She felt the tie—it was silk, so she tapped it and he ripped it off and put it in her hands. No watch. No wallet. She stood there with the tie, wondering what she could get for it. Not much. She felt the old itch but didn't scratch, too proud to do it in front of hm.

Stepping back, a little annoyed, delivering full attitude, she asked, "That all you can do? You run around town without a dollar? You allergic to help out folks?"

He took off the suit jacket. "Take this, it's brand new, it's a Coppley."

"Who that?" she asked, dubious.

"Cashmere. Lined. Look."

She looked. She didn't know much about these names but she knew fabric well enough. The jacket was soaking wet...but she touched it...soft and fine, the weave tight.

"How much you pay?" she asked. He seemed antsy, his cool going. Good. He was in a hurry, and that gave her power. The wind slammed into the porch hard just then, making the pink man shift his weight and look that way. "How much, I said?"

"That suit cost twelve hundred."

She whistled. 'Okay, he rich.' He pressed until she took it. Tan with white stripes. He put his hands on his pants, as if to say—you want these, too? She shook her head—she hated indignity. She'd suffered so much of that herself, what with her disease. 'Nought so strange as folks—so self-important just because you got a nice suit.' He stared at her. She let her eyelids droop and folded the jacket carefully over one arm and draped the tie on top. In her 'I'm the boss' voice, she said primly, "I take these. Pete's asleep."

She snatched up the bag of sweets. Then she gestured to the pink man and walked straight and proud to the big bedroom door and pushed the bell. She heard the man muttering behind her, "Thank you,"—he had strange manners, she thought—but she was already calculating how many hours until she could call Paw Pawn and get a price on this loot. The topical cream had run out what...three days ago? She could stop at the pharmacy on her way to the shop in the morning.

She pushed the bell again and left the stranger man. Risking a scratch, knowing she'd regret it, she climbed up to her bedroom to hang up the coat and tie so they would dry nice.

The Worm had worried about Sawdee Pete on and off from the beginning. After all, Pete's job position as a 'human failsafe' was his own creation, and Pete was his hire. Safety Specialist. He felt guilty for supporting Pete's tequila-drinking habit, now upgraded to fine mezcal—he remembered the only photo Pete had ever sent him...a wide-view glittering lineup of hundreds of imported bottles, Pete smiling crookedly among them in stud pose. It was Pete's way of reiterating he liked being at home—"Yeh-ah'm a home-body, under the radar"—he'd stated it over and over during the job interview; he liked staying up all night—"Yeh, night boy for me"; and he could still run fast—"Ran a 4.65 40 in college, no lie, look it up"—and, in the final interview, easily handled the manual valves and locks even with the bad shoulder: "Don't worry about me, Mr. Camel."

Pete must have sensed the Worm's anxiety; he wasn't just a big dude who didn't make it in the NFL. No, he was a man; the Worm abhorred the idea of exploiting him. He remembered taking him aside when he came in to H.R. to do paper work: "It's going to be boring, night after night, are you sure?" He felt proud how transparent he had been, but still...the guilt lingered, even now.

He barely knew Pete, really—two interviews, the hiring and orientation day, and after that...once a year for the unannounced emergency drill. (The Worm grinned: the year that jerk Terner started the betting pool, all he had to do is drop by Go Store on E Street the night before and ask, "What's Pete doing tomorrow night?" and Pete beat Terner's new young alternates. Pete had always scored below five minutes; though he was more haggard in the face and flabbier in the waist, he performed year after year, bets or no bets, young rivals or old, despite V.P.s who came and went and targeted Pete's salary as a potential boost to their annual bonuses.

The Worm campaigned tirelessly for Pete—"I'd say he's Pythos' most dedicated, reliable employee," and, "He's been here longer than you've been in the job market," and, "My safety practices, including his position, gives Pythos the highest E.P.A. ratings." He remembered cracking the smug look on the moronic Bendlam's face: "Before you eliminate his position, Mr. Bendlam, why don't you go ask Advertising if they don't mind changing all their copy to 'Second best.'"

So he shouldn't worry too much—the job remained perfect for Pete, and for years the Worm had protected it. The annual payroll report showed he only took three days of vacation a year, on average—the guy guarded the job fanatically. "What do I do?" the Worm had asked the H.R. head. "Well it isn't right to force anyone to take vacation," she'd said with a genteel tilt of the head. That was the last time the Worm could recall sending him a message: "There's no danger of losing your job by taking vacation or sick time." But Pete hadn't bothered to answer. So that meant the man was there right now, a few hundred yards from the plant, in his dark house, logged in, on-call, just as he was 362 nights a year. Drinking mezcal, most likely. Except tonight, the Guv was on his way to his door, with no warning.

He remembered finding a dead swallow chick beside fallen stones when he was very small. The horror was creeping up on him now as it had then. He'd run along a stone wall playing ball until he got to one end. He'd jumped on the edge until he'd broken away some of the stones. This chick must have been nested in the cracks between stones, and now it lay there crushed and dead, and he was to blame. This was the same. All the years of planning and protecting, but now Pete would be shaken into the open; he had to deal with the Guv face to face. Later he might be suspected, he might even be arrested, he might lose his job. The Worm hoped Pete was stashing away some of his annual salary in case.

The Worm checked the time. He felt the old pain along his pubic bone, but there was no way he'd take meds now. Better take a deep breath and stop worrying about Pete and the past, and start worrying about the end.

He scanned for a link and made a call. A woman's familiar voice answered.

Pete's eyes snapped open at the sound of the bell. What damn time is it? He flicked his eyes at the scan: system normal, 'shoooo' he breathed out. He checked his pager—nothing. He reached for the glass, empty; he refilled it and drained it—velvety smooooooooth. The bell rang again. He wasn't expecting nobody.

"What?" he called out.

"...Steadson, it's an emergency!"

What? Sounded like his position coach at Tech...sadistic mother. Some new boss man from the plant, a new inspection scheme, somebody from the board of directors-board of governors or some pile of shit? In a storm this time of night? Nah. He was pissed at the company—why's everybody messing with Mr. Camel? Also pissed at Na-re, she equaled right about zero when it came to screening people: couldn't she tell one line of business from the other?

"What you want?" he asked, unwilling to get out of his recliner.

"Are you Salty Pete? There's an emergency leak at Number Six, hurry!"

Unrecorded?!!!   Pete's   eyes   quick-scanned   the screens—nothing—before he bolted from the chair and was dressed in no time, just like the emergency drill. No warning, maybe the real thing—no problem, he was at the door, flinging it open, and looking at a guy whose ruddy face he knew from television and holy mother, not his position coach, it was the bad old governor of Texas!

Pat saw at once that Pete was drunk. He'd expected a fat guy for some reason, but Pete was a large, athletic-looking man in his 40s, a bit of a tummy, but clearly a man who lifted weights—his arms bulged out in that peculiar way that said, 'I could still play,' whatever it was he used to play.

"You Salty Pete?" The man nodded. "Let's go!"

"Yes sir."

They were out a back door and through a cyclone fence gate and running into a field, sometimes blown sideways into each other, and Pat had to push hard to keep up with the man's long stride—he must be six feet five inches. "Basketball?" he yelled at his back, partly to warn him he was drawing next to him. They ran side by side a while.

"Tight end." His voice came over thin and high for a man of his stature.

"Longhorn?"

The man spat. "Red Raider."

"Shoot."

Pete gave him a quick glance. "No coat?"

"Your woman took it."

"Not my woman."

"Housekeeper?"

"Shouldn't talk to strangers."

"Sorry."

It was an odd conversation, an odder dash in a lightning storm—not a good idea, against every lesson adults had taught him—but here they were winding through fields of pipes and wires and cables and beneath massive concrete tanks. Pete was fleet and sure. Pat fell back and mimicked his jumps, turns and dodges—it was not a set track—but he lagged more and more. He would have been far behind but there were several locked turnstiles to navigate that gave him time to catch up. Pete keyed them like a machine—slam in the tapered steel, turn, ching-open, get through, clang-close.

All the while rain pelted and Pat again felt like he was in another world—not hell but maybe some mythical land, like in a 60s movie, with the cold blue lights of an outdoor stadium, the blurring rain, the ugly faces of fat clouds roiling between the impossibly-large tanks. One of them leaking hydrogen. And then, also like in a movie, thunder boomed, seemingly right overhead, and lightning flashed, and for good measure a bolt cracked into a rod atop the main building.

By now, Pat was exhausted and could barely see. He simply followed the larger man's bouncing slicker. His lungs burned and, just as he was feeling the urge to vomit, a hatch in the ground appeared in the middle of a large pad of concrete. He staggered to a halt and bent over, hands on his trembling knees, panting. Pete keyed and spun the hatch open and, like on a hot night getting out of cool car, humid air steamed out. Pete slid down a metal ladder and disappeared. Dismissing the danger and nausea, Pat let his feet feel for each rung...there were many...and gingerly descended into the sultry interior.

It was painful and slow. By the time he reached the bottom, his thighs felt shattered and he collapsed. He looked around helplessly while Pete opened a lock box and extracted a large t-shaped tool. Then, he darted here and there...nimbly testing one station and then another. Rumbling noises all around might be machinery or thunder; the rain poured like a washcloth being squeezed out overhead. Pat was too tired to move. He pulled his head back and down, expecting a cataclysmic explosion any second.

As Pete continued his antics, Pat wondered why no alarms were sounding or warning lights flashing. It reminded him of movies showing a submarine control room on a routine cruise. But no depth charges here, he was below a leaking hydrogen tank!

Pete had put on a headset and was speaking to someone. And glaring at Pat like he was a criminal. He finished and put down the headset.

"Can you stop it?" Pat gasped, pulling himself up onto his feet. His legs felt like rocks were lashed around them. Pete didn't answer. He barked, "Can they stop it? The hydrogen? The leak?"

Pete's eyes blinked once and then stared. "Nothin to stop. Everything sealed up tight. Condition green."

Pat stopped breathing. "You mean...the lightning can't...?"

"No leak. No alarm on my remote. No alarm here, no alarm at Central," Pete said.

"Are...are you sure?"

"What kinda game you playin?" Now Pete was holding the t-shaped metal key like a club. Pat was astonished and couldn't speak. Pete started coming at him.

Miller was worried about Julia. Even though the airport was far north of town—and a total pain in the ass to get in and out of—he hadn't heard a word from her. He knew the flight had been delayed. The airlines had only recently added a night flight to San Antonio; grimly, he was amused—bad for business, this crisis. Still, Julia was probably safest just staying in the terminal; the winds kept increasing, and weather reports were saying the storm had a long way to go. Some cell towers were knocked over and thus service was spotty at the airport. What a night! Had the Worm studied meteorology or gotten lucky? Still, Miller liked to know things and usually made sure he did...but he had no idea where Julia was or if she was safe.

He didn't usually mind the office at night or long nights. He had all his gear, a refrigerator, and good tech. He didn't mind a crisis—keep the job stimulating. But he hated summer. He hated the heat, the kids everywhere. He liked it when hurricane season was over and everybody mellowed and thought about the holidays. Usually, he found storms interesting; but this one was really nasty. He was ready for this to all be over.

Anyway, he shouldn't be thinking about other times of the year, or Julia. He should be coming up with a better plan than the police chief and, most lately, the stupid interference by Homeland Security. "Can't we ship those people to Mexico?" one of the team had asked. "Not fair to the Mexican people," he'd quipped.

What next? The Worm was out of reach and the Guv had disappeared. Miller checked the distance—10 miles from here to the Pythos plant. Nobody in the office flinched when more thunder boomed and echoed; they'd all been fooled several times into thinking the Worm had succeeded with a demo charge, and now an explosion would probably be reckoned just more thunder. What a storm...

Pryor looked up at the neat row of gables and windows of Senator Mack's house. A curtain twitched and two eyes appeared, then a face, and then a woman's sleek body in lingerie. Lordy, what a night.

The curtain zipped closed again and, before he could turn off the engine, one of three garage doors opened. Were Mack and Feebee so tight she parked in the senator's garage? He cruised in. Then he shut off, gathered up his odds and ends, and slid off the soft leather seat. The garage smelled of damp dog food, but there was a hint of something else...fragrance...just a hint, like fresh mint plucked from an icy drink. He realized he was thirsty.

A light had come on when the garage door opened but now it clicked off, leaving him in darkness. He swore—why don't rich people have windows in their garage doors? He fumbled around and got his smart light on and shuffled over to the interior door, which was next to the water heater. It was the biggest water heater he'd ever seen. These were the people, he thought, staring at the monstrous thing, who used up more than their share of the kingdom. A noise startled him; the door to the house had opened, and the same woman he'd seen at the window was standing there, a filmy robe covering the lingerie he'd spied...a dusty rose color. But it wasn't the lace at the breasts that gripped his gaze like pliers on a wire casing, it was the eyes, sending invisible fishhooks across the narrow space between them. She was up three steps, he below with the key fob dangling in his hand. Caught.

They stood like that, exchanging invisible stuff, for what seemed like half a minute. A deep rumble of thunder outside the door was the only time her eyes checked away from his for a moment; when they returned, they were even more intense. He kept waiting for her to shift into polite speech, the way he'd seen her do on West Programming, with her eyes kissing, her shoulder slightly dipping, her generous smile lighting up the news camera. But none of this happened. She pulled open the door wider and stepped to the side. Pryor felt he had no choice...but to go inside.

Tanya wanted Pryor the minute she saw him despite the madness and danger of the moment. Not as tall as usually excited her, but intelligent eyes and youthful energy—she could see why Feebee liked him. Better in person than Feebee's photos of him.

She acted swiftly. She shut the door and said, "Change of plan. A bomb may go off. I got a tip on the bomber—it may be a hoax, but I want to check. I want you to drive me." She saw the look of surprise and—terror?—on his face. She had forgotten what she was wearing—so what, this was life and death. "I'm getting dressed. When I come down, I need an answer. Frankly, I'd rather have help than go it alone."

Pryor's mouth, which had been open, closed, and she wheeled and hurried upstairs to change clothes before he started asking questions.

Pat had been in scraps before, like the argument in the party meet up when the Lester brothers had both stuck their faces close to his and yelled, "You're full of shit!" And out of muscle memory and quick calculation, he had half-risen from his chair and head-butted the older one in the nose, slammed the younger's head into the table. Won that bout. A few times in his life, quick and decisive violent action meant success: the ultimate contingency plan.

And here came Pete, stronger than the Lester brothers (and armed), but Pat's brain quickly commanded his weary legs, and when Pete was at arm's length he bent his knees, pivoted, and snap-kicked the stronger man. He missed (high for the balls and low for the gut) and got a jolt as his heel struck bone. His leg sagged but he used his upper body to shoulder-cock and punch upward at the man's exposed jaw, bumping him and his weapon sideways...and smashing his pinky finger, which flared in hot agony. He aimed another blow for the kidney, but the guy bucked up suddenly and he felt his ear go cold and something skeletal said *crack*. Lights and equipment fuzzed and he felt the air go out of his lungs, followed by hard concrete against hipbone, neck twisting sideways, eyes smashed shut and not wanting to open again.

"Motherfuck," a voice was in his ear and he deduced that Pete had knocked him to the ground and was crouched over him, talking in his ear, which had felt frozen but now was on fire. "You no Guv. Who you really?"

Pat grinned—or tried, his cheek was smooshed against concrete—then tried to move his jaw, wanting to say, "The next president of the United States," but his jaw was stuck and his vocal chords felt like they'd been dried and beaten with rough rope. He summoned his strength and lurched and twisted—but his neck was in a vice and his head slowly, inexorably, inch by inch, was down-pressed against the hard floor again. He felt as if his neck muscles had been shredded. The rest of his body was in bone-deep fatigue, like during a bout of flu.

As he lay there with the big man twisting his head and bellowing, "Talk!" in his ear, a deep shaking made time seem to stick. Then there was a piercing alarm-like howl, louder than any concert or road equipment. It sounded like the warning for the end of the world. His head was free and Pete disappeared from view—the Worm had tricked them, lightning had struck or a real bomb had gone off! And what did anything matter? Pat heard Pete swearing and calling to God. So. Pat had to be the sacrificial lamb to save Houston. His body didn't have any strength left. The Worm had won his retribution.

As he lay there, he could see Pete limping in and out of his field of vision, while steam hissed and lights flashed and the ear-splitting blaring echoed. With a tremendous effort, Pat rolled over on his back so he could breathe more easily, and he saw Pete's backside vanish from the top of the ladder. While rain rained down on his face and blood ran down his throat, he prayed that God would forgive his sins.

Tanya didn't doubt the address Dennis had provided for the mysterious H.E. And she understood Dennis' warning that this might be the sociopath detected in the web messages. Should she tell Pryor? Her instinct was not to; she kept quiet and let him concentrate on driving. She was so glad to have company.

Pryor drove fast but competently, as if within minutes he knew her car better than she did. He didn't ask questions; he was focused on the road, his strong hands guiding the wheel.

The storm was particularly wild north of the Petro Patch; the unseen towers and tanks would be standing like targets for lightning, and the lightning kept charging and retreating as if the narrow Bayou waters were holding out but couldn't last much longer.

"Road's coming to a 'T.'" Pryor's voice startled her like a gun shot inside the car.

"Follow the GPS," she said. "You ever been in this 'hood?"

"No ma'am, never."

She hadn't either. The ominous name was 'Colonial Heights'. She felt her sympathy rise for them both, especially for Pryor—she was using him, putting him in danger. She would owe him, but she could pay later. She reminded herself Pryor could be an ally now and an enemy later. It was hard. She was used to the either/or political paradigm. But this crisis seemed to suck in everyone. Feebee hadn't betrayed her or her party just because she was dating a Whig. Tanya trusted Feebee to maintain confidentiality. And really, Pryor didn't have teeth like a shark, so...she needed him.

In her mind, she replayed the message from the Worm, warning her about H.E.: "Madame Senator, I don't want any explosions or deaths. But this man has said, 'Justice before mercy.'" She hoped for mercy.

She didn't like the justice threat. That was why she and Pryor were speeding to and from danger, for should H.E. decide to blow up half of Houston, as his media posts had insinuated, it might kill the Governor but the sociopath might kill her.

Lightning, on cue, struck a towering hulking building on the other side of the bayou, dancing about the blocky shape and then vanishing without a sound. Eerie. Pryor's hands gripped the wheel.

"It's not the first thunderstorm around here," she said as easily as she knew how. She put a hand on his shoulder, then withdrew it. Like the lightning, something crackled under her fingers and under his shirt. She didn't apologize. He looked at her—his eyes weren't scared but excited or...full of wonder, maybe?

"What do you think you're gonna do?" Pryor asked. He'd asked this before. She crafted a new answer.

"The Worm was vague. My aide thinks this bomber is for real."

"You got a gun?"

Tanya looked at him, amused. "I'm a senator. I'll use my tongue."

Pryor mumbled something about Sweet Jesus.

"Didn't Feebee tell me you got your degree in theology?"

Pryor's profile grimaced. "Divinity. Yes."

"Okay. Well, pray for us." She paused. His eyes shifted—intelligent, checking to see if she was sarcastic. "You're not a fanatic, are you?"

"I use my head," he said with a slight grin. "I can debate on people like you."

Keep ahead of him. She snapped, "And what about with people who set bombs?"

"I can debate with reasonable people."

"You meet many of them in your work?"

He shrugged.

The car hit a rut and the suspension snapped and groaned. "Careful!"

"Just a..." Pryor went silent, his mouth open, staring at her. She felt her hair standing on end. She looked out and lightning suddenly hit a cinder block they were passing, the familiar two letters of the company logo lighting up like in a commercial, and then a flash and hiss...and nothing. The car was still driving, Pryor's mouth was still open. They were still alive.

The car faded onto the shoulder—"Watch the road!" she shrieked, fearful that the lightning would miss them but they'd crash and burn anyway.

The **Worm** pinged but got no response from H.E. No response, and yet the signal hadn't been blocked. All had gone well enough so far, but the Worm was exhausted. Timing, always the problem. He ran through the escape route in his mind. He had never spent so much money on a 350-mile flight. Not for the first time he reminded himself he knew only about 10 words of Spanish. Maybe he should run the lingo app while he waited. Or he could get started out—at least clear the first door and wait in the corridor.

But he preferred the hardware set up to his smart. Smarts weren't as solid. He'd already had to change the connection several times. He sat and waited. This is what I'm good for, he thought. Sitting. With or without a margarita. In the sun or in the shade or in a bunker. In the dark. H.E. should have stopped the routine by now—past time Sawdee Pete would have found the false alarm.

Ping. 'Zeus one'. That was all, the message stopped, no punctuation. The Worm confirmed it was H.E. Good. He got set to go but then looked again, puzzled: what did he mean? Why didn't H.E. declare all safe? Zeus was the Greek god. All the calculations to assuage himself that no one would get hurt, but H.E. had always been unpredictable, and now what game was he playing? "It won't be enough," the guy had said at one point. Was he a hypocrite? A paranoid schizo? Why were these programmers so odd?

The Worm should move along the escape route, fly away, innocent, and yet...! 'One'. Were there more...more what?

The Worm found he couldn't swallow, choking-coughing. What did his body know that his brain didn't? The plan, had it been mangled? The Guv would think it was his fault. The plan had been sound except that it relied on others—what was that? Earthquake? The ground shook! He scrambled to bring up the outer cameras and in one corner, facing Lyonn, a smeary-blue plume filled the screen. He knew that tank, it was called Tallboy—it had opened like a raw eggshell cracked on a skillet, spewing its insides everywhere. Goddam. He thought of the Hindenburg as the tank's shell turned orange and skeletonized!

As the Worm watched, Tallboy melted completely and a spume exploded upwards! A series of ground-rattlings vibrated through the deep walls. Tanks were going up like matches in blue flame, one after another! The Worm had been betrayed!

Disaster! Anger and confusion and death, but no solution.

He couldn't do anything now, no one could, and if more lightning struck...! It was all in the hands of men who could walk and computers that could be hacked. "Hands," he whimpered. As if machines had hands. He looked at his useless legs. 'My dead limbs.'

A spectacular failure, betrayed by H.E. Pain spread from the Worm's spine, jagged arcs discharging agony into his neck and shoulders. His brain suddenly spun out of control. 'You're guessing! Jeering, coaching. Get mine. Being ours. Jasper. Huntley Dick-Read is on both our birth certificates. What? Flunking the PSIKE test. Putting down the stick. Do things. Not knowing how, they don't. But you know what's to be done. Give and take. Do and die. Stop dichotomizing. What the hellish? Gasoline. Methods are advanced. True. Toxic. But the equipment and the know-how. Phase it out. Don't say green. Could you say Granddaughter? Quiet! Burning sensation. Hello? Burning.'

Shaking, the Worm reached into his pocket.

Miller got to Camel first. He was obviously dead, mouth open, lips lined in a dry white crust. A stack of papers rested tidily in his lap, underneath a lidded-bin the size of a toolbox. Miller nudged the bin, pried the lid...watch, gold ring, belt. The watch and ring were too fancy for Camel. Miller nodded—the Guv's stuff. The other agents were snooping around. He put the lid back, replaced the bin. He glanced at the top sheet of the stack of papers—January 1, 1960—the guy's birth certificate? How odd. Underneath, however, was a bit of treasure: 'Unreported Safety Violations in the Petrochemical Complex of Houston, Texas.' McLain was next to him, looking at it, and Miller tapped it gently, and McLain nodded. The next page was a table of contents, listing dozens of petrochemical companies and safety failures, dating back 20 years. Chuw was at the top of the list. Lyonn was there, too.

Miller chuckled. "Whistleblower."

McLain said, "OSHA and EPA and Chem Safe Board gonna eat this up."

Miller was about to reply when the earth shook.

Pat smelled burning. They must be burning the fields—was it that time of year again already? He got that wild-free feeling of sky-wide possibility. Of running across the prairie—his legs ran, seeking buried treasure, swerving to beat the gang to the creek. The hawk, the fish, the other boys and the girl hidden in stalks or smoke or maybe they'd taken another route, the wrong track, the long way. Alone, night falls, which is why it's dark—and he's the only one who can get the treasure! It lies just below the surface. But he gets a vision of it that surprises him—not gold doubloons or black oil but something alive. A living thing—not Marta or his mother, someone else, not a feeling, not a tangible commodity—he strains to see but that's smoke and fire and agony, or maybe even....

Dull thuds, somewhere in the distance. Mouth tastes like charcoal. Was he in the sauna at the gym?

He rolled, pushed, sank. He panted. He pushed again, crawled. Something stabbed his palm. He recoiled and somehow, engaging his thighs, he found himself crouching and then upright. What? Oh yes. Shit, the ladder, the plant, the terrorist. Sawdee Pete. He couldn't go up the ladder, so he limped despite what felt like metal braces locking

his hips; he made for a flashing light and once he got there he aimed
for another and on and on through an endless steamy room. A panel
blinked and he poked at it and poked and poked and a door opened.
He shuffled forward, another door. He saw the night sky, saw mouths
move, arms waving, lights flashing. It was like in a movie with the
volume off. Like when he'd had that ear infection. He was eight or nine,
it was hot—end of summer—like swimming underwater in a pool. And
he didn't go to school—that's right, it was fall—and his mother had
hired a nurse, Ni Ni, and Ni Ni's stoic face came back to him, and her
voice singing—the words, she taught him the words, and he wondered
if he still knew them while people holding rifles were crouched all
around—a block of concrete in front of his tracks, but he just skirted
it and kept going toward the row of lights, and yes, he did know the
words:

> *Esperan los ojos*
> *A ver la eternidad.*
> *Y por eso, y por eso,*
> *No hay nadie feliz*
> *Y por eso, y por eso,*
> *No hay nadie, por eso*
> *Nadie sin la pena*
> *La pena*
> *En los ojos.*

Pat was reciting the song as some liquid rushed in from his left
and he hopped up on a walkway—a helicopter twirled overhead, its
rotors beating silently. He was humming or something, the bones in
his face rattled, disconnected, as if tongue and lips couldn't quite keep
up with the mind, and every muscle had to guess how to work, and he
remembered another voice, Ni Ni's daughter's, she sang too, Laura was
her name—they staged little concert dances, and it occurred to Pat that
Ni Ni must have been a dancer in Cuba before coming to Texas: ah, of
course, she wasn't a nurse like his mother had indicated, but a nanny,

and she'd stayed on that hot summer/fall, and by God if she and her daughter hadn't taught him Spanish and he'd forgotten it until now.

Why was everyone so excited? He was fine. And the Worm had faked it all! Bells and whistles but no leak. No leak. That must be water from a fire hose running on the ground back there. Yes, the Worm, Jon Camel, deceit to mess with him, a strange vengeance. But flashing everywhere were fire trucks and police lights and search lights. More music was running through his head—he hummed along, it was that big exciting Alleluia symphony.

Two large men hustled up in white hazmat suits and gripped him under his armpits and half-carried him some distance...away from that fluid, whatever it was, oh, yes, it must be water in case of fire or explosion or that stuff they put in fire extinguishers—like flying it felt, and then they were setting him down and people were hurrying him in the direction of a...an ambulance maybe—a van...or was it to a security checkpoint? It was like one of those trailers he'd seen movie stars go into. And all done in silence. They were getting out of the lightning storm, good idea. He felt himself giggling, muffled in his skull, as they rushed him to the stairs now on his own feet—he felt the flimsy steps vibrating with all the commotion, while his thigh muscles burned and his hip ached from the fall.

"Que cosa," he thought.

Inside the trailer were Tuck and Chambers and the police chief and a doctor, flapping their faces and he must've shaken his head...and the doctor was poking him and he didn't care, and Tuck was sticking his face in and pissing him off so he tried to say, "Get out of my face!" but the words came out in Spanish—*"Tumba eso!"* Yep, he must have voiced something, his chords and chest rumbled, and Tuck looked surprised. *"Me piro,"* he could feel his tongue trill, he tried to get up but they restrained him, the doctor was doing something with his ears. He tried to shout, "Sin pena!" but his tongue felt ragged and he wondered if the doctor had given him an injection because he felt no pain, he felt nothing, he floated and sank and stared at the metal wall of the interior of the trailer—or was it a van?—and he wondered if the Worm had fled, and he wondered: should he let him go?

Chambers steered **Don** away from the medical shelter and back to the car, barked a few orders into his smart.

When he was done, Don asked him, "Why was the Guv talking Mexican?" Don had never been so bewildered—the man he'd served for six years had seemed a stranger, a faraway look instead of the piercing gaze, talking in that slur-ry cheap accent.

"Spanish, Tuck," Chambers corrected him, looking up from his smart. "Who do you hang with, old geezers from the 1950s?"

Don shrugged—the smell of the anti-fire chemicals was still in his nostrils, his ears were still ringing from the sirens. He looked around at all the nonsense outside. "People are stupid."

"Say it," Chambers hissed.

"What?" Don asked, turning to look at his companion, whose balding head had turned red as a radish.

Chambers got right in his face and shouted, "Say it!" Don blinked. "Say it or you'll be done with public life in five minutes! This isn't 2016. This isn't 1950! We haven't beaten, 'Whig for Racist', right? Remember?" Don was reminded forcibly that Chambers wasn't from Texas—his East Coast brusque was aggressing all over the place.

"Say what?"

The old bastard smirked. He looked like a gangster. "Say why," he demanded over and over.

"Get off my ass, Chambers."

"I don't think so, not until you say why. Say why!"

"Why what?" Don burst out, ticked off the man chastised him when he was really just a handler, not a moral guide.

"Well, Tuck," the tone was softer but the words were thick and more like 'fuck' than 'Tuck'. "I ask you a simple question, Tuck. Why? Cause I can't ask you hard questions. Can't you answer a simple question? I ask you, Why was what you said wrong? You tell me. Or I swear to Christ you're done."

Don discarded the obvious sarcastic answers and then, pausing, realized this was his future—saying the right thing and getting tested—and it was going to take a lot of discipline to deal with it. Not only saying but learning and doing the 'right' thing. No more nights doing Em or Gwen or Reann or any other sexy woman like them. Well, he adjusted this grim future, maybe if he was *really* careful.

Chambers wasn't letting it go but shouting why a few more times, so Don obliged: "I said 'Mexican.'"

Chambers smirked. "So?"

Don visualized Em and then pushed her face away for Reann's fairer features, hair tucked behind her ears ready for business...ears, shit, what about the Guv's ears...what did the doctor say—some kind of hearing loss? Chambers was making a 'poofing' sound. Don waved him off, "So I shouldn't'a said 'Mexican.'"

"Why not, Tuck? What's wrong with Mexican, Tuck? Mexican isn't...? What, Tuck? Come on, big boy."

Don wished he could bite Chambers on the nose instead of answer. He folded his arms and in a mocking voice said, "Mexican isn't..." Shit, isn't what? It's a country. It's...right! "It isn't a language."

Chambers clapped. "And so?"

Yeah, yeah, he thought, here we go. Taunting Chambers, he asked, "And so...you think it sounds like I'm a...racist?"

Chambers thrust his face forward closer, "No, Tuck, it sounds like you're an ignoramus, also possibly a redneck, also possibly a total asshole. Is that how you want to present yourself, Tuck? To the party? To the American people? As an ignoramus and a redneck and a total asshole? You think that's going to get it done these days?" Don clenched his teeth together, afraid he might actually bite Chambers' ugly fat nose with all the fat ugly pores on it. The man's icy blue eyes sat low in their bulgy sockets. The guy was one ugly toad.

"Don't talk to me like that, Chambers," Don said slowly and pulled back, worried now about protecting himself. At that, Chambers' eyes drooped lower; the man looked predatory now. Don got scared. He hadn't noticed how big his hands were—they were slack in his lap, but they were a fighter's hands, scarred, deadly. Don mentally noted: use this guy and then lose him. "What's the plan?"

"The plan. The plan, Tuck. Is we get ready to accelerate." Chambers brought his hands up but instead of making fists cupped his own ears and shouted: "What if Steadson's hearing loss is permanent?" Louder, "You think a deaf guy can govern?"

Don's annoyance was punctured like a needle had injected him with euphoria. "Oh, shit." He looked at Chambers and grinned, tingles engulfing his insides like after the first sip of whiskey. "Oh, shit! Oh, wouldn't that be a shame?" He nodded and then beamed a big smile, sending Chambers a ray of excitement. "Keep feeding me."

Chambers popped him on the shoulder. "You better."

Don was delighted and tried to regain his composure. "So this Worm, this Jon Camel? He's some kind of liberal terrorist, right?"

"Registered Whig."

"Not possible."

"What the hell are you talking about. We have his card—thirty years. And he donated."

"No."

"Yes," Chambers said, wagging a finger. "Not much, but it's on record. Don't get confused about simple things like binary. You can't think no when it's yes. Can you."

Don was confused and said, "I guess not."

"You guess right. What we decide to say is something else. We. Not you."

Don considered. "Well, he's a pariah. A nut job. What a joke."

"But he's our nut-job, right?"

Don shrugged. "What do you want me to say to that?"

"I don't want you to say anything unless I tell you first." Don felt his collar prickling him—the prior delight and camaraderie gave way to anger; he wanted to punch Chambers' ugly nose.

"Well we can get this Camel guy for all this mobilizing for nothing?"

"If we can, we will, oh yes. Chuw is one of ours. Check their lobbies. What are you doing in your spare time, watching porn?" Chambers' tone was sarcastic. "Why don't you pay attention in future, Tuck? Ever heard of due diligence?"

"Uhhh, sure."

"I'll get you a list." Chambers looked at his smart. "Better get going, media will be let in any minute. Let's go shake hands with the hero."

Don straightened his tie and gulped. This was somewhat bewildering, but at least knew how to do that.

Pat stepped away from the podium—another speech, millions would see it, this time lauding a criminal and a political adversary: a Worm and a Mack. But he didn't care. 'Nobody's fool—' he said to himself and felt the ground wrench, accompanied by a dull noise like a quick zipper ripping open.

"What now?" he thought, almost laughing at all the equipment and hazardous materials vans and SWAT teams and people and lights and helicopters whirling around...but a helicopter spun madly and crashed to the ground. People sprayed in every direction like figurines in a cardboard box shaken by a giant. He turned in a circle, dazed—was it the second coming? Why did the helicopter crash?

Then he saw the geyser of pale blue fire. Hydrogen fire, he knew it: what if it spread down the row of tanks like dominoes, how horrifying—like the Gulf Oil disaster footage from his youth broadcast in color, with a red and smoky skirt beneath it and a shattered stem instead of a floating platform. And then he knew that the Worm had screwed them all over! Double deceit! And Pat raised his arms and howled in rage. Black smoke erupted and what looked like a black missile shot across the sky and where it landed orange flowers sprouted up and then more black smoke, agitated and fast billows ballooning and spreading everywhere. He felt a blast of hot wind in his face. More tremors, more smoke, more orange flames. Was this what people meant when they said 'warzone'?

A doctor was trying to do something, he shoved him into a wall. Someone stuck a message in front of him. 'We are trying to save your hearing.'

"I'm trying to save the goddam city!" he cried.

And he rushed out yelling for the police and the FBI and the TSA.

Miller knew the odds of a lightning strike on Tallboy leaking hydrogen weren't high. However, he reckoned it the tallest structure in the Patch. So there was that. Yet Tallboy had beckoned the lighting like open flowers seducing pollinators. As far as he could tell, there had been no thunder clap. Lightning was dancing south of them, but...not that close. Something stank, and maybe it wasn't the Worm; no demolitions in Jon Camel's record. Whatever the cause, a helicopter was already down, and flames and smoke could kill people, especially if this couldn't be contained. His mother's saying, 'One fire drives out another,' sprang up in his mind.

Miller ran briskly toward the governor, who was reeling away from the fleeing cluster of people, cursing and shouting and adding to the din of emergency vehicle engines firing and sirens re-doubling their noise. People seemed to be everywhere, and Miller knifed like a man threading through a riot, not looking left or right but straight ahead until he caught the governor by the wrists and shouted in his face with exaggerated lip movement,

"Get inside, we got a bomber, could be more explosives!"

And instantly, as the Guv looked him in the face, the ground shook as another explosion erupted and roared.

Chapter 5: Helium Ranch

When Pryor's fast car driving got her car within a half a mile of H.E.'s address, **Tanya** called.

"Wolf," was her aide's familiar reply.

"Go Dennis."

"Two things. One. Mr. Helium thinks he's very high I.Q."

Tanya felt her stomach burn. Old memories of college and the smart pride boys triggered a wave of fear. "What else?"

"Multiple bombs possible out there, not yet detonated."

"What?"

"Two or three total."

"Where?"

"No idea."

"Steadson should put Houston on lockdown. Shit. Thanks, we arrived." She clicked off.

Pryor glided the car over to the curb across the street from a metal security gate. It barricaded a short, narrow driveway fronting a single-story house. Visible through the thick rain was a sign: silhouettes of twin semi-automatic guns flanked by the words, 'No Trespassing'. Another sign was hoisted on the flagpole next to the single garage door: a lightbulb-shaped plywood notice which read, 'Helium Ranch'. The sign shuddered in the wind. The metal fencing ran around the perimeter of the property as far as Tanya could see. She had no doubt there were cameras, too. No intercom could be seen; nor was there any other way to get in.

"Do we jump the gate and knock on the door?" Pryor asked breathily, squirming in the seat as if he couldn't get comfortable.

Tanya hoped Pryor would be stable in a crisis. Had he ever been in one? She put her hand on his forearm. "Let me think." She felt his arm relax and turned to study the GPS image of the property. The Helium Ranch sat a dozen houses from a dead end, but what about at the back of the property? She used her finger to trace from the garage into the back yard, which in the sunny image sprawled grass and weeds up to the border of the state route. Was that a sprinkling of gravel, leading from the back of the garage toward the road? Was there a ditch between the road and the yard, or was that a piece of plywood over it? She wished she could ask Dennis—he could tell her when the image was taken and could zoom in somehow and test her theory. No time.

The same urge came up as when she spied on Steadson's hotel terrace—to jump. But that had been clumsy and dangerous and yielded little. If she was clumsy now, other people might die.

"First, this looks suspicious for sure," she said.

"You mean like a crazy white man lives here—yes." Pryor seemed to shiver. "Something tells me this is definitely it." Then he surprised her as he asked bravely, "Do we go in? Or get him out?"

Tanya thanked him silently. She thought a moment. She pictured H.E. inside that gate like an animal in a burrow. "What if we prod him so he runs?"

Pryor made some unintelligible remark—maybe something from the Old Testament. Then he pointed at the gun-flanked sign, "What if he shoots at us?"

"That could be bluff. What if he blows something else up?"

Pryor's hands were still clutching the steering wheel and seemed to be vibrating. Was he going to lose control? "Can't...can't we wait for...the FBI?"

"I don't want to wait," she retorted, frustration flaring—she needed the Pryor who was willing to help, not panic. She thought about it, though. The two of them were not mentally or physically equipped to break in. One thing was clear, and she said decisively, "Okay. First, let's block the gate." Pryor didn't move. "Pryor!"

"Yes, Ma'am."

Tanya calculated. "Turn so we're facing the other way. Pull up—it's narrow. And be ready to duck and run." She cracked both front car windows. "Pryor."

"Why?"

"It's a dead end!"

Pryor cleared his throat—not the answer he wanted probably—but he maneuvered the car into place in front of the gate. She felt a twinge of guilt putting him closest to danger. Then, without warning him—she didn't want an argument—she pressed continuously on the horn.

"What are you doing?" he jumped in his seat.

She laughed, a cloudburst of emotion pouring out and she felt better almost at once. His face showed complete disbelief. "Sorry—you jumped straight up like a cat." More honking.

"But what are you doing?" he cried over the noise.

She shrugged. "Prodding him."

Their eyes met but he didn't try and stop her as the horn blared on. They both looked at the house. A light snapped on somewhere in the back. A minute passed. She released the horn and listened. Was that a thump? Would the bomber raise the garage door and run them over, jacked-up mammoth truck tires crushing them? She honked again—a neighbor's light framed a window in dull white. She stopped. A quick flash of red beside the garage—taillights reflected! They listened: rolling tires on soft ground and the whine of an engine!

"He's gone out the back—turn right."

"Yeah." Pryor shot the car forward and turned so they were headed for the state route. A nondescript sedan, American-made, flashed in front of them.

"That's him!" Tanya shouted.

"Yeah," and Pryor cornered left at the junction without stopping or looking. The road was empty except the sedan in front down the long straightaway.

Tanya messaged Dennis. 'Quarry flushed. In pursuit northbound SR 10. Ford or Chevrolet sedan. Grey.'

"Nice," Pryor said.

Tanya stole a glance at him; to her relief, his manner had changed: his eyes were focused ahead but his body looked ready-relaxed, like when a dancer knows what he's doing. He was no good in a standoff, she thought, but he sure could drive.

On the long straightaway the gap between cars shrank. After a time, their man must have seen them or was confirming they were following because the grey vehicle veered suddenly onto a residential street. Pryor banked smoothly and accelerated. They were now close enough to see a head above the headrest lump, and she could make out the name Monte Carlo on the trunk. She felt satisfaction in having the faster car. The bomber veered again, down another residential street with the newer speed bumps, bobbing-slamming over each while her car gave-glided. Approaching the next intersection, Pryor blitzed almost to the bumper.

As if this provoked the driver into desperation, the grey Monte Carlo heaved suddenly and Pryor cried, "Sweet Jesus!", skidding to a stop. The bomber's car, sliding one direction and then the other, finally launched off another speed bump, balanced on two wheels, collapsed slightly, and then settled onto its side and crashed into the curb.

Tanya ordered Pryor to call an ambulance and jumped out and went over and looked through the cracked windshield, but it was impossible to see much besides a bunched-up shape. The car lay on its side, passenger-side doors facing upwards. Should she wait for Miller and the police to arrive? No, anything could happen—bombs could go off, tanks could explode! She climbed up on the car's side and waved aside Pryor's offer to help; she crawled and groped for the passenger front door handle. The door was undamaged and the latch clicked—unlocked. Her brain wondered idly why—maybe the crash system was programmed to let people get in. She pulled upward, fighting gravity and the weight of the door and with a surge of muscle (that Willie would have been proud to see), she yanked the door open. She peered down into the cavity and, as if at the bottom of a well, twisted around the steering wheel, a shape with glistening eyes could be seen.

"Are you alright?" she asked, flashing her smart light.

"Don't get closer, I'll detonate the airport bomb."

Tanya felt her heart stop. All sound ceased. Loo at the airport with Feebee. She should call, warn Miller, evacuate! Her smart light had illuminated a head cockeyed in angle to the rest of the body. Blood was fingering down the face in fine rivulets, but the eyes were watching her. It was a man, and he looked helpless, but was he? One arm seemed wrapped around the steering wheel like a sheet around a washing machine agitator, the empty hand limp. The other arm was hidden from view beneath him. She realized her eyes were dry and she started blinking, her mind mazing helplessly through dozens of choices that all led to 'detonate'.

She suppressed a rush of tears and tried to sound tough, "What do you want?"

"Call an ambulance."

"We just did."

"E.T.A.?"

"Pryor, arrival time?"

Pryor shouted, "Nine minutes."

"You hear him? Nine minutes until it gets here." This gave her an idea. "Can't I do anything for you?"

"Stay away."

She felt something—Pryor was touching her foot—would he climb up the car?

"He says stay away!" she rasped. Pryor retreated. She studied the injured man, wishing him dead, knowing she shouldn't give any ground, knowing she couldn't move or with a click perhaps he might kill. "I'll stay here until the ambulance gets here in case you need something."

"How do I know you've called an ambulance?" he interrogated.

"How do I know you've planted a bomb," she rejoined.

"Shouldn't play with fire, lady."

Fire. She knew this type. Flattery was the watchword, and definitely not humor. This is what Dennis had meant! The messages out there—some had been Camel's but some had been H.E.'s! How to play this man, the real criminal? Make it about him—like staying put in case he needed something. Flattery oozed out, just like when she was lobbying: "Well you've been impressive so far, I've got to give you that. Quite an operation."

"Chain reaction would have been better. You people got lucky." Which people—sane people? "The wind changed direction."

"Oh, was that it?" she asked, unsure how else to respond.

"This car wreck wasn't my fault. Driver assist should be banned. I don't need help turning a corner. This car tried to kill me."

Blaming the computer? She re-examined his position, the distance, wondering how a bomb was to be detonated—a smart most likely, but there might be some other device. She couldn't see a tool or device anywhere—she rested the light so its beam illuminated one side of the cab, mainly the windshield. H.E. was against the seat in partial shadow but she didn't dare re-focus it. Detonator, detonator...did he follow her eyes seeking it? Was that a smile on his lips? Or was the detonator back at his house and was he bluffing?

"You think you can outsmart me, lady, you're wrong."

She stiffened. "Oh, that's okay. I'm curious, why do you call your house Helium Ranch?"

"I used to own a ranch. Out west of Greens Bayou. They took it away. Developer and the bank forced me out. Knocked it down, cut down all the trees, built a housing development. They scrape away everything alive, that's what they do."

She was surprised how matter of fact this was. Logical. No bitterness could be heard—no feeling. So he was out for revenge against...? The capitalist system? Could she use that?

"You must have planned very carefully. So three bombs? Where did you plant the one at the airport?"

His eyes seemed to flicker and grow, as if they were candles turned on their sides. "You'll never guess."

"Probably not."

"Guess."

"Security?"

"What? Too difficult. Right over TSA would be a measure of justice, though.""

"Bathroom?"

"No! How many people are in a bathroom at any given time—fifteen? No, the Food Court. Shrapnel for dessert." He coughed up a wad of blood and stared at it, his bent arm moving slightly.

Tanya felt horror rising inside—how could she get to the detonator held in that bent arm? What likelier place for Loo and Feebee than eating a snack while waiting out the flight delay? She let the agony settle, took a breath, and smoothly asked, "Why should you blow up the airport now? Seems like you already succeeded what you wanted. Camel's dead. I don't see the point—you're not an evil person, are you? You knew all the emergency equipment would be next door at Pythos when..." She held her breath. The man was still looking at the blood on his chest. Maybe he would die before he could do anything! Was he listening? Could he still hear? His eyes seemed to have shut.

She wasn't sure if she should talk or not. "You just did what you thought was..." she floundered, but then she needed to talk, and the lies flowed, "You knew the lefties weren't doing enough, am I right? And the righties are ruining the state, yeah?" His eyes opened and he looked up at her, almost child-like. "Isn't that why you studied and planned?"

"Politicians, all the same," he replied, his tongue wetting his lips. "Scum. Say whatever they want. Long as they got power. No difference at all, one side. Or the other. Repeating the same lies until they believe themselves. Same tyrants over and over."

Was that a siren in the distance? Keep him occupied: "What do you mean?"

"Putin for Stalin. McClellan for McCarthy. T.T.C. for F.D.R. Steadson for Reagan. Better kill them before they kill everything alive."

Was he goading her into asking him why he did it? Was he a survivalist? Her brain didn't know—she didn't have enough information. Could she trick him? "But you don't need to do anything about the airport now, do you."

"I hate that airport." His voice sounded grinding now, as if his chords were covered in sand. "I hate the TSA." Another thought seemed to come to him. "Camel thought he was so smart, but he's going nowhere." Was that a chuckle or a gasp?

"Camel is dead—he's not going to the airport."

H.E. looked up at her—was he slumping a little? "Oh?"

"Suicide," she said briskly.

"Oh." He was quiet a while. Then, almost with a shrug, his voice continued, "He would. Coward." His bent arm was moving again.

Tanya had seen enough—H.E.'s hidden arm was death. She shifted her weight, rocked off her hands and knees and to a crouch.

'Plie and dive and grab his arm and take it away,' she coached herself, envisioning the choreography. She measured the distance—a dancer doesn't typically dive down. 'Quick and strong.' She was ready, but she would try one more time.

"But none of those men are at the airport. So it's not hurting them."

"Who cares, that airport is a shit-hole, full of shitty people."

"But my daughter's at the airport!" It just flew out. She had revealed her weakness, she had contradicted her own plan! Again, his glistening eyes looked at her. She continued, "Makes a mother worried."

Faintly, he said, "I hope you realize I'm not a mother."

"Well it does. Let me tell you about her."

"Oh God lady don't tell me about your kid." Something in this threat put her on the defensive. She had been ready to attack, to gamble, but the moment had passed, her chest was heavy. Time to defend—absorb his blows. "I hate it when people talk about their kids. Like kids matter more than the rest of us."

Tanya parried, "And my assistant. She's with my assistant. Smart young woman, got a bright future."

"Nobody's got a bright future," H.E. said, coughing again. "And don't start whining about sin. You people. So sensitive."

Tanya felt stung. How could this arrogant, smug monster...get away with this? Holding her and her family and Houston hostage? This blank face except for the streaks of blood, this flat voice tinny in the car interior. She realized something was wrong with her moral judgment of the man. She was certain he was a killer. But she couldn't calculate the risk of attacking him unless she knew more about detonating the supposed bomb. She had all the physical advantages, and there he was, winning. Flattery would only go so far. How to reach someone who doesn't feel? 'I know what not to do—don't threaten. But what do I do? Deal with him like he's a child? Remember,' she internalized grimly, 'His I.Q. is probably higher than mine.'

Okay. Okay, keep diverting him, keep giving him chances to brag. "Tell me how you planted the bomb on Tallboy."

"Oh it wasn't hard. I work there. I write the security software routines. It only takes one man to bring everything down, you know, if he's smart."

"I can't imagine it. Did you climb up and plant it yourself?"

He clucked his tongue. "I put it on a drone and sent it up that way. Easy as pumpkin pie."

'Except you fucked it up,' she thought, 'You only got a few tanks, not the whole row.'

His tone shifted, grew demanding. "What's taking so long, I'm getting cold. That's not good. You want my airport explosive to be on your head?"

She stared down at the bent arm—it was quiescent. She called behind her, "Pryor—E.T.A.?"

To her surprise, Pryor was almost in her ear. "One minute."

"Stay back," she commanded to keep Pryor from advancing. "One minute," she reported. "Sixty seconds."

"I'm counting," H.E. threatened.

What would H.E. do once it got there? Was that the end of her leverage and would he detonate? The airport might have opened or stayed closed—the lightning had moved south, delayed flights might be taking off by now—was that a jet plane she heard? Or car traffic? Somebody's dog was barking. What about the supposed third bomb—where was that and would it go off, too? She was panicking...

She tried to concentrate and reason out whether to attack or wait?—sirens could be heard—soon there would be circus here.

"Do you hear the sirens, sir?" came a question from her gut. No answer. "Sir?" Maybe he was dead! Passed out! "Can I get you anything?"

"I'm cold."

She suppressed a smile of hope. She forced out an offer, even though it would keep him alive. "I'll get you a blanket."

"Don't move. I have my eye on you."

She felt a twinge, then set her jaw. "Okay." The sirens were very near—she better keep pushing forward. "So is the detonator voice-activated?"

"Not bad for a Dem-Rep, how did you guess?" Bingo! "Senator Mack." What, was he flattering *her* now? "Too bad your party is too stupid to listen to you." She grasped that he enjoyed revealing what he knew...

"The detonator has to be something portable," she said on impulse. "While you drive. You just have to key in a sequence."

"It's voice-activated. Just two words," was his reply.

The target was the mouth, not the arm. Tanya felt every muscle in her body thrill like at the cue backstage on opening night: 'Places, please, dancers!' She realized she had been unconsciously watching H.E.'s breathing—to see if he was alive, no doubt—and she knew when his abdomen sank lowest. But this all happened at once inside of her—her body and brain had stood ready, and she was taking a breath in while he breathed out and bending her legs as she would for a jump straight down, and her throat was wide open and she was yelling to block any sound he might make and her arms were not in fifth position but a position her body invented—maybe a diver's—and her hands were open for one to hit his windpipe while the other punched/ covered his mouth, and despite wrist pain she pressed/clamped and she felt him fight for breath but she only exerted and yelled on, and when he went still she didn't believe it—possum—one hand clamped over his mouth the other driving his windpipe downward, tears or saliva messing his forehead while she kept yelling in the cramped upside down metal box with the killer beneath her.

Pryor was pulling on her arms but she resisted—she was bucking and screaming he wouldn't hurt Loo—but Pryor's voice was in her ear—

"Dead, it's okay, it's okay, he's safe—"

...and she saw/felt what death looked like in her hands, its stiffness, and she let Pryor have her arms under her armpits and eased her hands from the neck and face and then let her weight fall back on Pryor as he lifted her and she pushed with her legs, his chest supporting her as her bottom cleared the door opening. His arms were around her waist and they stood up together and as she turned to fall into his arms rough hands grabbed her and lifted her off the car, the memory of empty eyes staring, and she relaxed into this lift and floated down before banging her shin, but it wasn't Pryor it was the FBI guy and he looked crazed as he hugged her and thanked her and set her on a ladder that had appeared beside the car and to her surprise there were tears in the FBI guy's eyes. Then burly suited men were helping her down as she heard the reassuring—"Airport's locked down and safe,"—and she repeated 'safe' as firm hands steered her until, unsupported, she sank across the seat of a car, eyes catching lights flashing but the sirens were all silent in her ears, and Will would've said 'surreality', and she wished Will were holding her and that was her last coherent thought for a long time.

Chapter 6: After the Storm

Tanya wasn't sure what to expect from Steadson at the big press conference. Neither did Dennis or Jerry or Corvata or anyone else in the Democratic-Republican party. The Whigs didn't seem to know what to expect, either. There were rumors of dissension and Steadson, ever priding himself on being a maverick, might be headed for pariah territory according to some of the talk radio chatter. On the other hand, she reminded herself, the Whigs had a sneaky way of falling into line. Like her party had a sneaky way of screwing up their opportunities. The press had dubbed it, 'The Heroes of Houston Press Conference of the Century'. But Steadson wasn't her idea of a hero, and she felt more like a criminal.

She had three different speeches written. She had rejected the handlers and their drivers and their offers—she told Jerry to get off her property when he rang her doorbell; she was proud she hadn't let him in. Alone, in her car, with a single motorcycle escort, she looked at her destination: the bowels of The Summit parking lot. She'd been here once as a girl when it was an indoor sports arena—bio-dad had insisted they see the basketball team win the title. Now it was some generic megachurch. An aptly surreal venue for a joint press conference held by the Texian conservative governor and the Texian liberal senator. There had been an explosion and damage but it had all been contained. 'A narrow escape,' the press called it. No shit.

She was in a blocked off section of the parking structure and maneuvered behind the escort until the rider waved her toward a parking spot, which she nosed into. Her hands felt tight, and as she took them off the steering wheel sharp cramping pains jabbed in both thumb pads. The escort saluted and idled. She turned off the car, gently lifted her case, nodded at the escort, and got out of the car and over to the elevator. Like in an old movie, a 'boy' welcomed her, and pushed the button, and rode the elevator up with her.

She had to stay in the present, whatever might happen in the coming months. She thought back to yesterday's video call with Steadson. He'd let her video-join the psych evaluation of the Worm. She remembered the music of the woman's accent as she explained that, like a good game player, the Worm had followed a well-planned strategy. She enunciated clearly that she had analyzed his communications and separated them from H.E.'s and, in conjunction with Steadson's eyewitness account, concluded that, when assembled together in the correct order, the Worm's strategy was to graphically demonstrate the safety threat to Houston and effect change by getting the governor himself to look at the big picture and the immediate danger of a single tank on a single petrochemical plant. Not to cause an explosion.

"Mr. Camel was meticulous in practicing deception. But he was just as careful not to tell any untruths. His watchword was 'justice'. On the other hand, his colleague, the man called H.E.—"

But the lawyers had interrupted and told her with the criminal case pending and Mrs. Mack on the video-call, it was best to shut the heck up. Tanya smiled at the memory. Steadson, reading captions, had reacted a few seconds later by lifting a thumb and nodding.

Were there really signs that the governor might change course? He was quick to thank and blame. But would anything really change? What was 'justice' for the ecosystem? Wasn't that the bigger question? She had woven this view of justice into two of her speeches. It was an interesting word, loaded with meaning and subject to subjectivity. Steadson and his cronies were afraid of it. They wanted justification. She took a deep breath, trying not to get tangled up in labels and rationalities. People could be so turned off by logic and pseudo-logic. Being right was such a pain in the ass, she thought. Everyone wanting to be right. And then, how did retribution and forgiveness figure in? And mercy? The personal vendetta between men—would it play out like the last war?

The elevator doors opened and the young man gestured down the hall. She thanked him and stepped out and the elevator doors closed behind her. She was in a foyer. Reflexively, she looked for the restroom and went inside. Empty. She went into the last stall. She peed. She looked at the *Times* article which detailed more of the psych report on the Worm.

"His 'threat' messages point to the threat posed by industry to the health of Houston's people and its environment; according to Camel, the petrochemical companies are the criminals. He listed the threats as short-term and long-term. Most threats he called lack of proper safety protocols. Other threats he cited as long-term destroyers of the environment and people's health. These reference the toxins and pollutants released by petrochemical manufacture and the lack of any way to dispose of plastic waste.

"The other set of messages were personal. They indicated Camel was afraid the earth was doomed unless people took extreme actions to save it. He cited the high rates of cancer among residents in Cancer Alley. He used the governor's celebrity to get out his message. He surrendered documented proof of dishonesty, bribes, and safety breaches among the petrochemical companies' leadership. He also ended his own life.

"He doubted his gambit would work, that it would get the governor to change his mind about these issues; he predicted at one point only a 20% chance. And that, he said, was worth his life."

The *Times* editorial had been more pessimistic: 10%. Other outlets had weighed in, like prognosticating a sporting event. Dennis had even told her there was a website that provided betting lines on the likelihood of all things political—from senate races to likelihood of bills being passed. That website had put the betting line at 15% chance The Guv would reverse his State Energy Policy.

So, what was her prediction? Whatever, she'd grudgingly come to respect the Guv. Surely Steadson would take credit for stopping the

Worm. He would hype his presidential bid. He would downplay her actions against H.E. He would call for her to stand trial for murder and when the coroner's report was made public what would the legal interpretation be? What did the percentages about the Energy Policy matter? He'd find a way to let them all go back to business as usual, maybe with a few more safety measures. But Steadson help save the earth? If she had to pick a number, 18%.

In other words, an 82% chance of no action and ultimate climate disaster...her fingers floundered trying to get the toilet paper off the roll. Disaster. Murder. She bowed her head, hands on her knees, sitting on the toilet seat. Death. She had killed someone. To protect her baby girl. She pictured Loo eating ice cream and the bomb detonating...but it hadn't—she and Feebee made it, oblivious of the dangerous explosive in the food court until after they'd landed in San Antonio. Oh yes. The airport bomb was removed. The Gulf hadn't turned toxic in a matter of minutes. The storm had blown itself out. Outside The Summit, the sun was bright.

Outside this bathroom stall, in the aftermath of the crisis, among thousands of people, with millions watching, Tanya would confront Steadson. She forced herself to get off the toilet, wiped her face, and flushed.

The V.I.P. antechamber was jammed. The route into the arena ran past the Governor, beaming tall in the crowd like a rock in whitewater. Somehow, he knew she'd entered because he waved, his face animated. She smiled mechanically; unlike her, he enjoyed attention, he thrived in the limelight, and this was *his* big event. Camera operators and microphone wearers and even pen and paper reporters and autograph-seekers and self-important whatnots eddied around him. She recognized many of them. How deaf was he, she wondered, as they talked and gesticulated at him? Was he immune to this thunderous din? Two harried-looking lackeys stayed near him as the rest of the crowd flowed.

Suddenly, Steadson broke off and waded over to her; the crowd undulated and in a few moments he was in front of her, shaking her hand. Flashes flashed. She smiled, knowing that backstage was really onstage; in fact, she glimpsed herself on a monitor that likely was projected into the arena. Steadson was saying loudly, over and over, in Spanish: "This woman saved Houston, Texas, too." One of the lackeys kept translating this into English every time he said it in a high-piping drawl. She had heard a rumor, but it was odd hearing Steadson speaking Spanish. Meanwhile, the other lackey, a confused-looking young man with freckles and a ruddy face and neck, his hand clutching a tablet, also seemed unlikely; he must be able to flash what people said in text in case Steadson couldn't hear (or lip-read?).

She wasn't sure whether she should try and talk to Steadson—it seemed impossible, even though she wanted to ask him just what the fuck he was going to do at this big event. He was saying something else in Spanish that Tanya couldn't translate right away—the verb tense was unfamiliar. The translator, his Adam's apple bobbing wildly, chimed, "Goodness could save us all."

Was Steadson creating some distance, some space, to work? A funny idea considering the crush of people. She was looking at the back of the governor's head now as he'd moved on to more hand-shaking —she'd missed her chance to say anything as bodies created snags between them. She could see some grumpy faces along the walls, including the Lieutenant Governor. The guy had declared both the Worm and H.E. liberal radicals; she wondered if he'd get a gag order from his party like she had from hers; he seemed to say whatever came into his head. This led to the thought—Steadson's party doesn't know what he's going to say today! They look worried. She wanted to feel elated but she was worried, too. She realized she had better ask him to his face what he was planning to do before she found herself on camera on microphone in front of millions. Maybe she could whittle her speeches down to two. Boldly, she crossed into the wake of a large woman and pivoted so she was next to the Guv; he was talking loudly to a cluster of reporters about golf of all things.

"Governor," she said in his ear, tapping him on the shoulder.

He turned and joked, "No hablo con el diablo!" Faces registered laughter and annoyance in equal measure. A suit jacket shoulder boxed her out; she recognized Lieutenant Governor Knobs, thrusting out his hand between her and Steadson. Miffed at first, she was mollified when Steadson would not shake the man's hand.

"That wasn't nice," Knobs complained. "Now why wouldn't he shake his Lieutenant's hand?" He kept asking this, over and over, loud enough for the journalists to hear and record—smiles faded and bloomed around them. "Maybe I'll run for President!" A smattering of hoots and clapping.

A handler appeared and grabbed Knobs by the arm, pulling him back while he shouted, "Fire me, Guv, fire me! Oh, he can't hear, he's deaf. Oh, no, how will a deaf man govern?" The handler pulled him farther aside. It was like a game of basketball under the rim, everyone scrapping for a rebound, the crowd of reporters recording it.

Amidst this confusion, a dapper woman wearing a headset tapped Tanya's arm and took her by the elbow—Tanya cast her as the referee, calling timeout. The woman shouted, "Almost time to go in." Tanya nodded and allowed herself to be led toward a waiting area, with a monitor and speakers, large stuffed chairs and a low table. The woman spoke in a reassuring, clipped style that said, 'Capable and Efficient'.

"Good morning, Senator. You will be taken in to your seat in the arena in about ten minutes." She pointed at the monitor and Tanya could see the onstage seating—burnt orange on one side, sickly green on the other. Yuck! "You'll sit upstage of your podium. The governor will speak for about twenty-five. You're up next, you get five." She got close to the monitor and jabbed a finger. "Your podium is orange and to the right of the governor's. A warning light will flash when your time is up. Stay at your podium, he'll join at his and we'll do a Q&A with

Media first and a few general audience. The moderator will tell you when to answer. Don't worry about camera position, just look at the Governor or at the audience. Questions?"

Tanya thought for a moment. Her questions were too big for this woman. "No."

"Please wait here, I'll come get you in ten. Coffee? Water?"

"Valium?" Tanya joked.

"I have Tylenol," the woman replied humorlessly.

Tanya withdrew into her own shell. "I'm fine," she said.

The woman moved, hurrying without rushing, closing the door and leaving her in suspense.

Steadson appeared hunched, and his voice was overloud as he leaned near the punky microphone: "My fellow Texians!" There was a loud cheer, the metallic echoes of the building reminding her slightly of that basketball game from long ago. Not, of course, as hysterical as when the Rockets won it all and her bio-dad embraced her more joyously than he ever had before or since. Tanya clapped politely. She and this man had eaten watermelon together and weathered a crisis. Yet, she reminded herself, he was like her dead father: a friend only fleetingly.

"The other night during the lightning storm, I went to hell and back. To hell. And back." He was speaking a little loud and flat, but not bad for someone who was now, she was told, pretty much deaf. "I wasn't the only one suffering. I know many of you here in Houston suffered mightily. And then there was the bomb at Lyonn. Home-grown terrorism. Seven people dead. Millions in damage. Fortunately, the fires were contained. They didn't spread and cause a bigger catastrophe. Fortunately. Thank God. Now I want to make it clear that the man known as the Worm—he wasn't the bomber. He made threats but those were a hoax to draw me in. He didn't plan to blow up anything. No, that was the work of his associate. A dangerous man named Hal Ernon. His job was to make the hoax look real. Unfortunately, Hal Ernon made it real. We are fortunate that Senator Mack tracked Ernon down. Very fortunate. She stopped him before he could explode a second bomb at the airport. She stopped him."

Steadson gestured Tanya's way. Applause; she felt her cheeks glowing.

"About the third bomb. I know there are stories out there. Ernon claimed there was a third bomb. We believe that was a deception. Ernon's dead, of course, so we can't say for sure. We don't think so. But we will remain vigilant and we welcome any information about it from anyone.

"But the Worm now. He was not after deaths. Oh no. He was after me. He was after my conscience. He took extreme measures to warn me about the dangers at Lyonn and other petrochemical plants. As has been reported, he took his own life—that's between him and God. Lyonn wasn't diligent about safety. That's why it was so easy for the terrorist to plant his bomb. That's on Lyonn. And, it's on us in government. God may choose to punish the Worm. But I promise you that I will do everything in my power to see Lyonn takes responsibility for that lack of safety. For the deaths of seven people. I promise you, Lyonn will be punished."

Applause. Curious, Tanya thought, that he named the corporation like it was a person.

"Yep. But that's not enough." Silence. Pause. "My fellow Texians." Uneasy pause. "And my fellow Americans. We survived this crisis. But we are facing an even bigger one. And we all know it deep down."

'Here comes the presidential candidacy pitch,' Tanya thought. She mentally moved her second speech up to first. Either that or he was going to come after her now. She arranged her third speech to second and braced herself.

"This crisis is so big. So big a lot of us don't even see it. It's a problem we keep pushing off until later. But that's not the American way. The American way in a crisis is to get after it! The American way is to look it straight in the eye and take it on. And get it fixed. And we can do it. We can fix it. Therefore, I am going to declare a state-wide emergency." Tanya realized she had stopped breathing. "Hal Ernon's bomb misfired; it was supposed to start a chain reaction of explosions. If it had, we'd have suffered another Hiroshima here on American soil. Thousands of lives lost; billions of dollars in damage. Compromised the entire Gulf ecosystem for decades. My fellow Texians and my fellow Americans, we got lucky the bomb didn't work right. Lucky. I don't like living on luck.

"Therefore, by executive order, we will shut down all petrochemical plants in Houston until they pass stringent EPA and Chem Safety Board safety inspections. Until these companies clean up their acts, and make safety a top priority, they will not go back online. That's my promise."

Scattered applause.

"And that's only a start. Now, I don't know how many of you folks know about the day of tears." Tanya wondered if the Guv had lost his sanity along with his hearing. His party bosses must be cringing! "Well, a day of tears is what we almost had. A funeral for Houston and the Gulf. And to tell you the truth, I don't want to see our people of Texas suffer like that. It just about happened, and if we don't change our ways it <u>will</u> happen, some day. But we can stop it. We can. I say no day of tears in Texas. We are in this together."

'The earth is a gift to pass on,' sprang into her mind, Willie's voice, quoting that book. Did Steadson know the arena was hushed? With his hearing loss? That everyone, including Tanya, was in suspension, like a communal held breath?

"I am going to propose legislation to change the State of Texas over to Safe Energy by 2050." Ahhh, she thought, 'safe' energy...not 'green'! A new brand for the Whigs? What was 'safe' exactly? Or did that matter? It was a step! "Safe Energy to keep us a great state. And I want you all to get behind it. So you and your children and your grandchildren...are safe. Forever!"

Steadson was nodding and beaming.

'So we have a future,' he seemed to be saying, holding everyone rapt in that vast arena. "Safe Energy," he repeated. "We got options out there. We got good energy companies and we got good manufacturing companies. It'll take time. It'll take innovation. It'll take money. But we got all those things right here in Texas. Right here in America, by God we do. And in the end, this is a win for everybody. Safe, long lives for all. Thank you, and God bless you."

Measured applause. Steadson waving. Voices. Commotion, people leaving, people entering. Steadson sitting down, nodding and beaming still as if losing his hearing had increased his facial expressions. No mention by the Guv running for president! No bid for votes!

The dapper woman was signaling Tanya. She was so surprised she realized there was no introduction. She went to her podium among the confusion in the place—some cheering, some booing, some yelling, dissonant clapping, seething chatter. The governor of Texas had either just committed political suicide or outflanked everyone. What should she do? The Guv could lose his corporate backing, so running for president would be difficult. 'Is he sacrificing himself?' Tanya asked herself, awed. 'What do I say?'

Out there in front of her, the undulations of people, lights...the arena where basketball hoops and hardwood had been replaced by choir platforms and a generic altar...well, it was like a dream. Would song break out in this monolithic space, heralding a new day without tears? Was Steadson baiting her into a political trap? Was it all a scheme to drum up Whig publicity? It sure didn't feel safe.

And she'd killed a man. Soon, one day, when the coroner report was made public, would that make her a villain? Mixed up inside she felt insecurity, frustration, optimism, even elation....Who would have thought that it would take a man like Pat Steadson to break her shell?

None of the speeches would work, that much was clear. Steadson had broken the fucking mold. She had to speak. She got close to the microphone. How long had she been standing here? How did she look? What would her critics...? No. She felt everything slowing down and she ignored the bank of cameras, letting it all recede.

She cleared her throat as the bubbling and panting conversation continued. Loudly, she announced, "My name is Senator Tanya Mack." A strange buzzing echoed about the cavernous interior—some kind of silencing cue, she guessed. It worked.

She paused and then she just started talking. "This is an historic day. And I am proud to be here to see it. Let's have a round of applause for the Hero of Houston."

In the car, waiting for the traffic to ease up, Tanya listened to Loo's complaints over the car speakers. Loo hadn't cared that Mom had just been on television. She cared that one of her cousins got more cookies at dessert and that the flights home kept getting delayed. Also, Loo 'hated' San Antonio. Furthermore, she said Auntie couldn't cook, Feebee didn't listen, and she wasn't allowed to sleep in the big bed. Tanya told her she'd be home in the morning, the flight had been confirmed, and that she should get the most out of her visit, even if she didn't always get her way. Loo grumbled that they might be going to the mall and a movie, which would be okay maybe. Tanya told her she envied her going to the movies.

After she disconnected, security gave her the go-ahead and she started the car and exited the lot. She turned on LNews, blah-blahing about a man saving a child named Agate from a wrecked car. She was thinking 'Agate' a strange name and took a quick look at the screen—a man flexing biceps, suspended behind a close-up of the girl's face—she was only about six—eyes wide, smiling as if in great relief.

Past the gate, Tanya's car entered the dusky evening. To her amazement, there was no traffic jam—somehow, in the last hour, the 16,000 people at The Summit had dispersed. Maybe out front there was still a media buzz, but this back exit was nearly empty. She saw a few police, a few arena security, and a man standing at the end of the drive. The profile was familiar—the broad shoulder, tight against a dark t-shirt...a longing arose just as she identified Pryor. He turned his head. Instead of pulling into the street, she idled and powered down the window.

"Ride?" she asked.

He stood for a moment, dark sunglass lenses revealing nothing. Then, he glided over to the passenger door and slid in. How young he was in many ways—the smoothness at the corner of the eye, the fine hairs running along the teardrop earlobe, the bare, prominent cheekbone, the patch of scruff on the front of the chin. Ten years age difference seemed like a lot more now than a few weeks ago. He faced her but, before he spoke, his gaze was arrested by the screen. The news story about Agate was still going; Pryor squinted at it and then took a sharp breath in.

"What?" she asked. "Do you know that little girl?" He cleared his throat but didn't answer. "Do you know that guy who saved her?" Pryor's free hand shot out and smacked the console, jarring off the screen as it switched to the radio. A distorted keyboard riff played. "What's wrong?" she asked. He seemed all wound up. Was it about the press conference? Or the trauma?

"I came to tell you," Pryor started but then he stopped. His lips were pursed tight.

"Were you inside?" she asked. He shook his head.

"I streamed it. Everything's crazy," he said. "You know it won't take."

She shook her head, smiling: "The thing is broken wide open." He made a scoffing noise. She said quietly and deliberately, "It's the most hopeful thing that's happened in my career."

"The Governor will be kicked out and then he'll be just a deaf man wandering the panhandle."

"How tragic," she replied.

"And you..." Pryor trailed off.

"I'm gonna run with it," she said.

"We broke a commandment," he said after a while. Did he mean running H.E.'s car off the road? Or her stopping the terrorist from detonating the bomb by stopping his breath? That coroner report...H.E.'s injuries and prognosis before she got to him...

"Go on," she urged, feeling reckless.

"I don't know," Pryor said.

She kept challenging, "What did you come to tell me?"

"Can we drive?"

"Where to?" she asked. Then she joked, "I'm not a taxi service."

"Yeah," he said, "That's my job."

She didn't know if he was going to befriend her or blackmail her. The word blackmail, the fear of something else wrong, pierced her—and yet, after a moment, it seemed to pass right through. It smarted but she didn't mind it. It was diminishing already. She was alive, she could do hard things. She realized she didn't care about what happened to her. It was Loo and Steadson's granddaughter and young people like Pryor and Feebee and the nanny and all of them, all the younger people coming up behind who needed her attention. Steadson had broken the stony wall and the secrets were running out into the open. Maybe there was a chance.

"How about my place?" she asked.

"Yeah," he said.

She felt a little thrill in her belly.

On the radio, the keyboard piece had ended and a ZZroux beat replaced it, a cool voice crooning,

Score it up

Women and men

He get nine

She one outta ten

Tanya felt warmth spreading from her belly throughout her body. Pryor's arm was so close to hers; they had been together in this car during the chase, and then there was the wreck, life and death. And now their arms, just inches apart.

She put the car in gear and drove over the limit. She didn't care if anyone saw them or followed. It was the dance version of Score, playing up the on-ramp, down the off-ramp, into her neighborhood, so cool even as she slid into the garage. When she powered off, the singer hiccupped and fell silent. The car felt close and quiet until Pryor shifted and the seat sighed.

"Everything's crazy," the young man said, looking straight ahead. He was shaking his head. "I prayed on it, but....Crazy!"

He wouldn't look at her; she thought this was a prelude to something unpleasant, but yet her body remained warm and ready. Maybe her body knew better?

"Like a prayer answered but not what you expected," she said gently. He still wouldn't look at her. She wondered if he would ask her straight out if she had actually strangled the terrorist in the car. Didn't he know how deliberate she'd been? But there was something else in his shyness. What were the rules now? "Come inside," she said and got out of the car.

Fussing with the safety belt and the door lock then fumbling closing the door, he said, "I could call a cab."

Not definite. She always took charge against a 'could'. "You could come inside," she insisted, getting excited that he would.

His nostrils widened slightly. "Who's at home?"

Her eagerness increased. "Nobody."

"Shouldn't get seen with you."

Did he mean Feebee? She teased him: "Does your Party spy on you when you're on the job?"

"Hah..."

She saw his gaze flicker. Sent. She guessed Pryor had been sent to get info on her. She had tried to be a spy and a heroine, but just now she was merely an aroused widow. She was betraying Feebee, but she wasn't pruning a potential marriage. Well. If he'd been sent..."No spies here, " she said.

He hesitated next to the car, as if reluctant to leave its security. "Everything is a joke with you."

They weren't an easy couple for sure except animal chemistry. Really, she thought, I could let him go. The worst danger was past and there was plenty ahead. There was nothing noble about desire, she reminded herself, it simply existed. Right now. She moved toward him and he crossed his arms, either closing her off or fighting his own desire. She saw his throat quiver as he swallowed.

"Pryor. Listen."

"Better not."

That halted her. She wanted to say they wouldn't be jams... She wasn't sure of the best word—she didn't like the phrase 'play solitaries'.

Finally, she whispered, "Just come inside."

She hoped for a yes and she also hoped for a no. This young man had his life ahead. He could still be a decent preacher, relaying sententious messages to a nice congregation in a mid-size town. But a party member? A lobbyist or a weasel? No. He could drive fast, he was strong enough to pull her out of that wrecked car...but...he was too nice and....too honest.

When it came to round ball, would her bio-dad have cut Pryor? Conceded he'd be a nice bench player? Dad said she was cut out for the bruising struggle in the paint; Ronnie was only good for an unmolested jump shot. She craved a tight clutch with this man, still hesitating, arms flexing as if he was getting ready for a weight-lifting rep.

"You okay?" she asked.

"No," he answered.

No, wait, she was asking the wrong question. Just now she didn't care about Pryor's feelings, the future political ramifications, the next term in D.C., her day in court. She cared about fucking Pryor, and he wanted her, she could feel it along her skin, her neck prickled. She imagined him naked, his belly touching hers. She was ripe, now, it was time, her body said so. Could he sense that, too? He licked his lips—because he was thirsty? Hungry? His body was talking to her...

She cut right to it. "Pryor, want you."

He shifted, arms slackened, head back, and then he turned and gazed into her eyes; breath rushed into her lungs and he made a slight gasp as he leaned in and pressed his lips to hers. What a kiss.

It wasn't long before their clothes were a hindrance and they tumbled through the garage door into the sitting room, clutching each other and kissing—his lips were delicious—trying to remove belts and straps and work free buttons. They must look silly, she thought fleetingly, but this was replaced by a renewed urge to get all his warmth all at once.

She stretched and ripped while he cradled the small of her back with one arm and supported her down to the plush carpet whose ivory color always reminded her of Yasha's fur. The thought of the dog's silky fur was replaced by a surprising reward as his fingers found an untested place and, with increasing speed, unexpected shivery pleasure.

A surge of competitiveness ensued, and she used his waistband as a lever to twist him sideways but couldn't get him on his back. He retaliated by lifting up on his arm, now held to the floor beneath her weight, but she managed to roll him again to the other side until they settled side by side. They kissed and she took hold of him starting low and, as he tensed, she glided him but kept hold, reminding him with every twitch of her fingers that she could do anything she liked. He fought this a while, putting a hand down, which she swatted away, and then trying to mount her, which she thwarted with a warning squeeze. She made tight-quick thrusts, which she modulated by clutching his chest and pinching the flesh. He responded and they found the right tension and settled into a smooth rhythm, side by side, an unfamiliar position to her body, but, looking into each other's eyes, they kissed with their looks, slowly building a harmonious beat until, not able to keep her eyes open, she let sight go and, wrapping tight to him, embraced and tilted and clutched and released and released....

Later, she stroked his eyelashes, then his brows. As she sensed him drifting, she blinked tears, purging herself of the last few weeks, and let her arm drop limp on his rising and falling flank. She tensed up a moment, ready to despair or run or fight. She wanted to run away and fly away, to Hawaii or somewhere...but she had escaped with Pryor for a few minutes, and she was home. Safe, in the bed in the dark.

She surrendered...tears flooded...followed by an image: Loo's hopeful dark eyes and smiling face.

Under hot tears, her cheeks stung...so she took in a deep breath, and another, and her eyelids eased and her eyes rested until they were barely open, following a distant solitary light—she sighed hopefully—toward peace.

Acknowledgments:

"Oedipus Rex" by Sophocles; The World Without Us by Alan Weisman; GURPS Infinite Worlds; Wikipedia; Debbie Hunter; Factfulness by the Roslings; The New Quantum Universe; The Meridian Encyclopedia of the Second World War; How We Decide by Jonah Lehrer; Braiding Sweetgrass by Robin Wall Kimmerer. Cover Art Work by David Nez.

About the Author

Connor lives in Portland, Oregon. He started writing poetry at the age of 11, and his first published poetry book was Image Made Word (1990, Roan LTD).He got up the nerve to start e-publishing novels in 2020, and the following titles are available: The Hero of Houston, an eco-thriller; Measure Her, a comedy-romance; Blue Blossom, a historical memoir set in World War II; and a sci-fi/fantasy trilogy, The Three Books of Wisecraft series.Premieres of play adaptations of Jane Austen novels, Persuasion and Northanger Abbey, were produced by Quintessence: Language & Imagination Theatre, where he was Artistic Director. Other productions of his plays include: Pride and Prejudice, The Child is Father of the Man, Face Reader, and Treatment (Quintessence); A Bawdy Tale (Montgomery Street Players); Zaney (Arts Equity); I Go to War and Vaward of Pallas 3 (Epicurean); The Folio (CoHo) and Where No Storms Come (Stark Raving Theatre).He is also a director, having received his MFA in Directing at the University of Portland, and he taught acting for 24 years. His book Imaginative Doing, Collected Essays on Acting was published in 2013.